PUFFIN CANADA

THIS IS ME

After graduating from Queen's University, Stephanie Craig travelled abroad and taught in Japan for three years. Now living in a small town in Ontario with her husband Daniel, and his daughter, Tyler, she teaches Grade 7. *This Is Me* is her first novel.

This Is Me

Stephanie Craig

PUFFIN
CANADA

PUFFIN CANADA

Published by the Penguin Group

Penguin Group (Canada), 90 Eglinton Avenue East, Suite 700, Toronto, Ontario, Canada M4P 2Y3
(a division of Pearson Penguin Canada Inc.)

Penguin Group (USA) Inc., 375 Hudson Street, New York, New York 10014, U.S.A.
Penguin Books Ltd, 80 Strand, London WC2R 0RL, England
Penguin Ireland, 25 St Stephen's Green, Dublin 2, Ireland (a division of Penguin Books Ltd)
Penguin Group (Australia), 250 Camberwell Road, Camberwell, Victoria 3124, Australia
(a division of Pearson Australia Group Pty Ltd)
Penguin Books India Pvt Ltd, 11 Community Centre, Panchsheel Park, New Delhi – 110 017, India
Penguin Group (NZ), cnr Airborne and Rosedale Roads, Albany, Auckland 1310, New Zealand
(a division of Pearson New Zealand Ltd)
Penguin Books (South Africa) (Pty) Ltd, 24 Sturdee Avenue, Rosebank, Johannesburg 2196, South Africa

Penguin Books Ltd, Registered Offices: 80 Strand, London WC2R 0RL, England

First published in Viking by Penguin Books Canada Limited, 2002
Published in this edition, 2003

2 3 4 5 6 7 8 9 10 (TRS)

Copyright © Stephanie Craig, 2003

Manufactured in Canada.

NATIONAL LIBRARY OF CANADA CATALOGUING IN PUBLICATION

Craig, Stephanie, 1971–
This is me / Stephanie Craig.

ISBN 0-14-131399-4

I. Title.

PS8555.R317T5 2003   jC813'.6   C2002-905196-7
PZ7

Visit Penguin Books' website at **www.penguin.ca**

Special and corporate bulk purchase rates available; please see
www.penguin.ca/corporatesales or call 1-800-399-6858, ext. 477 or 474.

To my mother, Barbara, for her constant support
And to my father, John, for his undying encouragement
With love

This Is Me

Chapter 1

This is me. It's a picture I drew of myself for my English class. We are talking about perceptions of people and how we see ourselves. It's kind of interesting. I guess I see myself as pretty happy. And as you can tell, I'm no fashion queen.

I'm thirteen years old. I just turned thirteen last week. So now, as my dad says, I'm *officially* a teenager. I'm in Grade 8 and this is my final year at Millcreek Senior Public School. Up until a few days ago my life was pretty dull. But I have always enjoyed listening to my friends talk about their lives at home and school. In my group of friends there are some who are already dating and others (like me) who just listen and watch the continuous cycle of going out and breaking up.

I wouldn't call myself attractive but I've always wondered if someday I might be discovered. It is one of my daydreams. I guess you could say that they, my daydreams, take up most of my waking hours.

I try really hard not to daydream in math class, but it's tough. I try not to because our math teacher, Mr. French, is my dream teacher. He knows exactly how to make us quiet but he is also really nice. I'm sure it helps that all the girls are in love with him. And with a name like French when you teach math, you have to have a sense of humour.

Back to my daydreams. I have quite an imagination and I can spend hours just making up stories in my mind, from my wedding day to my funeral and all things in between.

My name is Shelagh and one of my main concerns right now is that for the rest of my life I will be correcting people about the pronounciation of my name. It should be Shey-la but each year, at the beginning of school, the teacher calls out, "SHEEELA Howard?" and I always respond politely with, "It's Shey-la. I'm here."

I suppose I could wear a sign on my shirt or have a special one printed that says, "My name is Shelagh and you say it SHEY-LA!" I wonder what my friends would think of me then.

The thing about being in Grade 8 is that there really are so many things going on in our lives between school work and friends and what's going on at home. It seems much more complicated than it ever was before. In Grade 7 it *seemed* like life was full of things to do. It was busy and adventurous. But thinking back it now seems like life in Grade 7 was a breeze. It was easy, uncomplicated and fun.

Now the teachers keep saying they are preparing us for HIGH SCHOOL. If life is all about getting ready for the next stage, how much fun is it ever going to be? My older sister is in Grade 10 and all her teachers ever say is "We are trying to prepare you for university."

Oh, well. I think I'll be okay with all this new stuff because I'm a pretty good student. I don't usually get into trouble unless I have a giggle fit, which happens every now and then. When it happens it's like some force has taken over my body and there is nothing I can do to stop it. I've made a few teachers almost lose their minds trying to get me to stop, but I really can't. So I've left the room a couple of times and gone to the bathroom to collect myself.

That's really my only problem in the classroom. Well, that and daydreaming. But most of the time the teachers don't notice my daydreaming.

There is a guy in my dreams. He is older by a couple of years and he's very handsome but he is mysterious in that I can't see the details of his face. I can tell that he's extremely kind and soft-spoken and sometimes we dance in my dreams. He is a great dancer and we usually just float around like our feet aren't really touching the ground. Well, mine aren't anyway.

That's one of my favourite daydreams right now. I think it's because I'm hitting puberty. We've been talking about it in health class but to tell you the truth I'm not really sure what it's all about. We get these badly photo-copied handouts of pictures of boys and girls but it's our insides and it's hard to figure out exactly what it's supposed to be.

I can imagine what it's all about *on me,* but since I have limited experience (read *no experience*) seeing boys naked I find it almost impossible to guess how it all works. There are all these veins and stuff going this way and that and I know they are inside the body but it's still hard to imagine.

I guess I should tell you about my family because it's a bit of an interesting story. I don't really know many people who have "normal" families, well, except for my cousins. My aunt and uncle are so in love. I guess it's kind of nice but I'm not sure that my cousins appreciate how important it is.

I have an older sister who I already mentioned. Her name is Jane, which she hates. She thinks it's really old-fashioned. She can be really mean to me when she doesn't want me around but generally she's pretty cool.

I like listening in while she talks on the phone with her friends. She doesn't have a boyfriend yet and it's kind of a sore spot with her because *all* her friends do. She's pretty, though, and I wonder if the boys are too afraid to ask her out.

I have a little brother too. He has cerebral palsy, which makes his muscles not work properly. He is the love of my life. He's seven years old, his name is Jake and he is the sweetest person in the whole world. He will do or try anything and doesn't seem to be too concerned with the fact that everyone stares at him whenever we go out.

Then there are my parents. They are both kind of out of the picture, believe it or not. My mom left us when I was about nine, I think, and moved in with some guy. I don't remember a lot of it, I mean when she left, but I remember bits and pieces. Now she lives alone and we visit her every so often. We don't have a regular schedule like some of my friends, but that's fine because I prefer to stay at home.

My dad is at home, sometimes. That is when he can get away from work. I get pretty angry when we have night after night of sitting around the dinner table without him. He missed my birthday party entirely and never really even mentioned it. I let it go but it still makes me mad.

The big thing that makes all of this okay is that we have a housekeeper and she also doubles as a nurse. We are not rolling in money or anything but Jake needs to have someone look after him pretty much twenty-four hours a day so Betty has become our surrogate mom. I love her and basically think of her as mom *and* dad. I do as much as I can to help out but sometimes I just feel like being on my own.

My bedroom is my haven. I have pictures cut out from magazines and photos that I've printed off the internet of my favourite actors, actresses and singers. I put them all over my walls and my dad rolls his eyes when he sees it but doesn't say anything. I have my own room, which is really important to me. It's not big, but there is enough room for my single bed and a desk and of course all my pictures.

I have a schedule of things I'm supposed to do to help out Betty and I'm usually pretty good about getting them all done. Sometimes I just feel like being really bad, like all of a sudden surprising my dad by not doing what I'm supposed to. The problem is Betty is the one it would end up affecting, not my father. I guess it's normal to feel like you want to do something crazy when you are angry with someone.

So that pretty much sums up my life at school and at home. But there is more to tell.

Chapter 2

The story of my life picked up a few days ago when my friend Tanya Miller asked me to be involved in a great idea that she has been thinking about lately.

Tanya, believe it or not, has seven brothers and sisters. I know it sounds crazy but it's true. I've seen them! They're mostly half-brothers and -sisters because at some point Tanya's mother and father, who both already had a few kids each, met, fell in love, got married, had two more children of their own (Tanya and her little brother) and now they all live together.

She has become a pretty good friend over the past year and I feel good when I'm with her. We met at the beginning of Grade 7, but this year we've already spent a lot more time together. She's one of those girls who's really confident but not rude about it. She makes you feel like she actually likes being around you and isn't going to up and leave if a better friend comes along.

First I should explain that Mr. and Mrs. Miller run a retirement home and Tanya and her family live on the main level in the back of the building. Tanya is really good about it all and often helps out with the seniors. She says it's fun to play card games with them and has learned how to play all kinds of old games that *I* certainly have never heard of. She knows all the seniors by name and especially the details about who has how many children and where they all live. It's pretty amazing to me that she has spent so much time getting to know them. Other people might think it's strange to see a thirteen-year-old girl who *wants* to spend time with older people like that. Not me! I think it's great!

So this is it. Tanya's brainchild. She wants to have a student volunteer club where every member would be paired up with a resident of the retirement home and there would be visiting hours every week. Tanya says it would be great for both groups because we can learn a lot from them and they would have young, lively visitors coming to see them.

Last week Tanya and I had our first club meeting. We were the only two there but we made lots of plans. Tanya made herself president and me vice-president. At first I was nervous about the idea. I've never really been a *leader* before. Now I feel good about it and the more we do, the more I like the idea of being *vice-president*.

We also made posters—lots of posters—letting everyone know about the club and how to join. The posters said to get in touch with either Tanya or me, if they were interested in joining.

During our meeting we also chose a name for our club and talked about our teacher sponsor. Our club's name is "Match Made before Heaven." We were worried that it would sound a bit morbid, but Tanya says most of the residents aren't sick or dying, they're just old and are totally at peace with the fact that they aren't young things any more.

In order to be an official club we have to have a teacher sponsor who would be willing to attend meetings and other events. We need to approach someone who is most likely to agree and I think we should ask Mr. French. That way we would never have to worry about recruiting new girls to the club and we know we'd have fun. And a bonus would be that we'd get to talk to him, look at him and generally spend more time with Mr. French.

Tanya and I have had fifteen students approach us because of our posters. Most of them are girls but I think there are about three boys. I'm pretty sure they are doing it just to hang out with the girls, but that's fine because they'll still be part of the whole volunteer thing.

Tanya and her parents sat down after the meeting and chose fifteen seniors to be matched up with. They were those who didn't have a lot of family coming to visit them or who'd recently lost someone close to them, that kind of thing.

At the next meeting, in a week, we'll let everyone know who they're paired up with. Tanya and I are planning an introduction party to be held in the common room at the retirement home. Her parents have been really helpful about giving us ideas and telling us what kind of food we should plan on having and all that stuff.

The next thing we need to do is convince Mr. French to be our sponsor. I asked Tanya if I could do the asking because, well, I'm sure by now you know why. She said sure and good luck.

Chapter 3

When I arrived at school the next morning, I walked straight into Mr. French's room. I had a job to do and I was quite excited about it. To my surprise, Mr. Crane, the principal, was sitting talking to Mr. French. I had barged right in on them without even thinking. I slowly backed out of the room, excusing myself and trying not to blush.

A few minutes later, as I was waiting in the hall, Mr. Crane came out and nodded to me in his official principal way. I edged my head around the door frame to see if I could catch Mr. French's attention without embarrassing myself again.

"Hey, Shelagh. Come on in."

"Hi, Mr. French. I'm really sorry about that before. I didn't realize you were busy."

"That's okay. We were just discussing the upcoming

staff meeting and getting some ideas down. What brings you in so early today?"

"Well, you know Tanya Miller. She's in class 8B?"

He nodded and said a very faint, "Mmmh hmmm."

"Well, see . . . sir, you see, she has this amazing idea for a new club and I've been helping her out with it. It's the best, sir. Honestly. We already have fifteen students who are interested and I'm sure there will be more if we can get the word out and become an official club. The thing is we need a teacher sponsor. And . . ." I finally paused to take a deep breath. "And . . . I was . . . well, *we* were wondering if you'd be willing to be our teacher sponsor." I smiled my best, warm, caring, student-asking-a-huge-favour smile. I had one hand behind my back with my fingers crossed and was also thoroughly enjoying my time one on one with Mr. French.

"Well, that was quite a pitch. Can I ask you a few questions about the club?"

"Yeah . . . uh, yes, of course, sir." I hoped I would know the answers.

"First of all, during that great little speech you left out what kind of club it is to be."

"Oh, dear. That's the best part! Tanya's family runs a retirement home and basically we want to start a volunteer group of students. Our goal is to match up students with seniors in the home and have visiting sessions with them. The students will come ready to listen, to learn and to play cards or whatever is on for that visit. We've already come up with a name but maybe you'll think it's a little too much." I hesitated. After all he'd only asked me one question.

"And the name is . . . ?" he said with the grandest of smiles.

"Oh . . . ha, ha . . . well, it's called Match Made before Heaven. We thought it was kind of cute, I guess." Oh, God, now that it was out of my mouth it sounded awful.

"Hmm. I like it. How much time would each student be required to commit?"

"We've decided that one hour a week would be the average time. Students can either come for a one-hour visit or if they'd prefer they could come for two half-hour visits. I guess it really depends on each person's individual schedule." I was trying to read his mind. Was that too much time? Was it too little? But honestly his smile was seriously getting in the way of my mind reading and I had to give up.

"Well, it sounds very ambitious. I assume you're bring-ing this to me so that I can pass it on to the PTA as well?"

I couldn't tell if he was annoyed at my asking for that or pleased to help.

"Well, sir. Yes, that was what we were thinking. That is if you think it's a worthy idea and you would be willing to support us and act as our sponsor. We plan to have weekly meetings every Monday after school for about half an hour. We'd need you to attend those meetings but you wouldn't have to come to the retirement home because each student will be attending whenever it is convenient for her or him. Of course we'd appreciate it if you could come to the introduction party when all the students meet their partners for the first time." I was rambling again. He'd only asked a simple question.

"No problem. It's settled then. As long as it passes the PTA council you will be an official club, with me as teacher sponsor and you and Tanya as student representatives. Would you be able to sit down with her sometime before tomorrow and get the whole idea down on paper?" He smiled now in a way I thought I understood to be genuine interest. He liked our idea.

"Of course, sir. We'd be happy to do that. We'll write it up as an official proposal. Thanks, sir. We, *I* really appreciate it." And I did. Crushes are hard to bear and I was starting to think it might be even worse now that I'd be seeing more of him.

"We'll see you this afternoon then, Shelagh." Ahhh, and he even said my name properly.

I couldn't wait to tell Tanya how well it had gone. Well, I'd be sure to leave out the part when I forgot to tell him what kind of club it was.

Chapter 4

That afternoon I explained to Tanya how well things had gone and we'd sat down to draw up our proposal for the PTA. I was pretty sure that Mr. French would give it his best shot at the meeting and sell our idea to all the members.

Tanya was starting to get really excited about the whole thing and we were beginning a temporary list of volunteers and their partners. After we dropped off the proposal to Mr. French, Tanya told me she had someone special picked out for me.

"Her name is Dorothy," Tanya smiled as she began to describe my new partner. "She is eighty-two and in pretty good health. Her doctor says that her heart seems to be quite weak but you'd never know it from looking at her and most importantly her mind is totally clear. The thing is that her husband, Frank, just died a couple of months ago and so she's new in the home and I think she misses him a lot. Can you imagine spending almost sixty years with someone and then all of a sudden he's gone? Anyway, her children come to visit her fairly often but they are really busy with their own families. She is a grandmother of six and a great-grandmother of two. I just think she's really special and has a lot to say to someone who's willing to listen. So, Shelagh, I thought you'd be a great match."

I was really touched that she'd seen me as a good listener and excited too that she'd taken the time to pick someone special just for me.

We decided to take a break from pairing partners and wait until the morning to find out how the PTA meeting had gone.

Friday morning was the day of reckoning and I arrived early again hoping I'd be able to find Mr. French and see how it had gone the night before.

"Shelagh," Mr. French came in the front doors of the school right behind me.

"Oh, hi, sir. I . . . . How was . . . ? Uh . . . hah!" I took a deep breath. "Did the meeting . . . ?"

"Come on into my room and have a seat and I'll tell you all about it." Luckily he cut me off before I could make a bigger fool of myself.

Mr. French explained to me that he had made copies of our proposal for every member of the PTA and that he had discussed, over the phone, the entire idea with Tanya's parents. He wanted to confirm that Mr. and Mrs. Miller were in on the whole idea. Then he ventured out to the meeting with all the weapons he'd need to win his battle.

He told the parents and the other teachers that we were good, hard-working students, that the idea had come entirely from us and that we'd already begun the foundations for the first meeting and matching.

As he was reviewing the meeting, I realized that he had a shiny gold band on his ring finger. Why had I never noticed that before? Now I'm not so naïve as to think that my crush would ever be more than that, but it was a bit of a jolt to my daydreaming life to know that there was a woman, and a very important one at that, in Mr. French's life. And it wasn't me and never would be me.

I was starting to feel something in the pit of my stomach. It was a twisting feeling that I did not like and I wondered for a brief moment if it might be jealousy. No! I wasn't in LOVE with him or anything. I just liked, you know, to be near him, talk to him and look at him.

"So you'll be pleased to share that information with Tanya then."

"Pardon?" He'd jolted me back to reality with this possibly very important and potentially good news.

"I said you'll want to share the good news with Tanya I suppose." Mr. French had a quizzical look on his face.

"Oh, yes, absolutely! Maybe I'll send her in when she arrives at school so you can tell her in person." Brilliant! I was now sure that the news was good but I wanted clarification that *everything* was a go. "Thanks so much, Mr. French. We'll see you at the meeting on Monday after school."

I was trying to pull myself together, act like I had been listening the whole time and appear professional in our new joint venture.

Tanya arrived in the playground only a few minutes before the bell was to ring and I had to tell her that I was pretty sure we'd got it but not entirely. How silly did that sound?

"Well, what'd he say?" She was looking at me like I was completely off my rocker.

"Umm . . . well . . . I think it'd be nice if you talked to him yourself and he can tell you all the details of the meeting without me making a mess of the recap." I hoped she would buy it, although I guess it didn't matter if she knew I was so enthralled with him I couldn't even listen for more than a few minutes without my mind wandering.

She agreed to run in ahead of the bell to see if she could catch him before first period began.

Later in the morning we saw each other at opposite ends of the hall and she gave me a double thumbs up. I let out a huge breath and realized I'd been holding my shoulders high with my fists clenched all morning.

After lunch our first official announcement on the P.A. system reminded members that the first weekly meeting of the Match Made before Heaven club would be held after the weekend on Monday at 3:15 p.m. in the gym.

I was glowing. I could actually feel it. The funny feeling in the pit of my stomach was gradually changing from a tight knot into tickling butterflies. I was proud of us, what we'd done so far and totally excited for the future. Some of the hardest challenges still lay ahead.

Chapter 5

I arrived home feeling satisfied that together Tanya, Mr. French, the other volunteers and I would accomplish good things.

Jake was lying on the floor in the living room and Betty was getting dinner ready. Jake's head rolled towards me and he started to grin like a Cheshire cat. I wondered if he was happy to see me or if he had something else up his sleeve.

I soon discovered what he was grinning about. He had his paper, paints and paintbrush on the floor beside him. Jake, despite his disability, had incredible creativity and willpower. He would try anything and do his best to be good at it.

He rolled back to his painting and gingerly picked up the brush with his right hand. His fingers twisted awkwardly around it and his arm moved in jerky strokes.

Despite this he created a beautiful mix of colours in circles and stripes. They looked spectacular. With a lot of therapy and hard work he had managed to learn to paint.

He really amazed me sometimes. How did he know which colours would look good together? I never have had the knack for that. He must have been born with it.

I went over to him, kneeled down and gave him a hug. I asked him if I could have the painting to put on the wall in my room. He nodded his head in three exaggerated movements and then smiled and groaned a greeting of hello and welcome home. He was starting to say something about Dad when Dad opened the front door. Jake grinned and rolled some more with this exciting news.

Dad being home in time for dinner was like a little miracle in our house. I was really happy he was there because I wanted to tell everyone about the club and everything else that went along with it.

Dad came over and picked Jake up and gave him a big hug. Then he leaned down to kiss me as I got up off my knees.

"So, guys, I decided enough was enough and I left. I simply up and left work. I think they were all staring down my backside but for some reason today I didn't care."

This made me smile. My dad was like that sometimes. Once he decided on something he wouldn't go back and change his mind. And I loved that about him. It didn't happen very often, but when it did he seemed so cool. I smiled at him and he smiled back.

"Okay, it's all ready to go!" Betty yelled from the dining room.

Dad put Jake in his chair and attached his tray to the front of it.

I looked around and realized Jane was still in her room, probably on the phone. I left my chair, went around the corner to the bottom of the stairs and hollered for her. Jane was never just sitting around in the living room before dinner. She would never *waste her time* hanging out with the family.

I went and sat back down, Jane arrived and Dad said grace. It was a rare occasion because, like I said, Dad was seldom home for dinner, but whenever he was we clasped our hands and bowed our heads. I liked the ritual of it, the routine, the memories of when we were little and the idea that this is what a family should be doing before dinner on any given night.

Betty was the best. She made food that looked good and tasted good and even though it was seriously healthy it didn't taste like it. She always sat with us for dinner and would help Jake in any way that he needed. That usually meant wiping his mouth, for although he could feed himself, he often missed his mouth.

As we were finishing our meals the conversation turned to me and Dad asked what I was up to at school. I started to explain about the club and I went on and on and on. I knew I was rambling but I just couldn't contain myself any longer. Dad continued eating while he smiled at me and encouraged me to explain to my heart's content.

And I did.

When I finally finished with a rebroadcasting of our afternoon announcement, he flashed me a huge grin and clapped his hands.

"Hurrah! Hurrah!" he shouted.

I can tell you for sure that Jane and Jake were looking at each other as though Dad and I were nuts but I didn't care. I wanted so badly for him to think it was a good idea. Now I could tell him about it all as it went along. Every step of the way from the first official club meeting to the partner match-up party and each visit with my own partner, Dorothy.

As I thought of her, I said her name. I told Dad and everyone that Tanya had already specially picked out someone for me to be partnered with.

"That's great, hon! I really am excited for you." Dad seemed truly pleased.

Jane said something under her breath about my being a "goody-two-shoes." I glared at her, vowing to myself that she would not ruin the excitement I felt about the club that Tanya and I had worked so hard to create.

Jake was too busy eating to let me know what he was thinking, but I knew that if I explained to him later what it was all about he would at least think it was cool.

As Betty and I were clearing the dishes from the table she gave me a knowing smile and said that the idea sounded wonderful. She said she was really happy I was going to be involved in something so new and exciting.

Truthfully, I think she worried about me. I've never had a very large group of friends, just a few close ones that have come and gone over the years. Betty had mentioned to me a few times before that she wondered how I was doing, socially she meant. I always tried to reassure her that I was happy enough, but ever since Mom left and Betty came to live here, she's known that I'm not the most outgoing person in the world.

I knew from the expression on Betty's face that Match Made before Heaven would provide her with the relief she needed with respect to me and my life. I would be meeting new people, spending more time with Tanya— who Betty thinks is a good influence—and I would also be expanding my horizons by spending time with an eighty-two-year-old woman.

As I washed the dishes and she dried, we talked about the club, the other members, Tanya and her family and, of course, my new partner, Dorothy. Betty had heard bits and pieces during dinner but she seemed quite content to hear it all over again. And, as I'm sure you know, I was more than willing to share it over and over again.

Later that night as I was falling asleep, Dad poked his head through the door of my room, which I had left a little ajar. He asked in a whisper if I was still awake.

"Yeah, Dad. Come on in." I rubbed my eyes a little but I was pretty sure I hadn't been asleep.

"Well, my sweetheart, I just wanted to tell you how proud I am of you. It's not every day that you get to see your child take something on, pursue it and then be successful as well. I'll tell you it feels really good to see you excited about something."

"I know, Dad, and I am. I know too that it's just the beginning and things will probably get more difficult for a bit before the visiting really starts up. But I really enjoy getting it all organized and being in charge and having people come to me to find out about what's going on. It feels good."

"Well, don't let it go to your head but I'm sure you'll make a great leader."

"Thanks, Dad."

"I love you, sweetheart. Don't let the bedbugs bite."

"I love you too, Dad. Thanks."

He quietly walked towards the door and closed it without even a click.

I couldn't get the smile off my face and I must have fallen asleep like that because the next thing I knew it was morning.

Chapter 6

All weekend I felt renewed. Talking with my dad and his telling me how pleased he was really made for a great time. My mind was clear and focused and I had a goal that I knew I wanted to reach. As a bonus, it was going to be FUN!

Monday arrived too quickly and I had butterflies as soon as I awoke. Tanya and I had spent Sunday afternoon finishing the matching of partners. We made information cards for all the students about their new partners that included their ages and hobbies. We also planned in detail our first official meeting.

It had gone really well, the planning that is, but now that the day of our first meeting had actually arrived I felt fear and turmoil. I questioned why we had ever begun this in the first place. I knew deep down why, but I wondered how I'd manage to get through the day.

All day teachers were telling me to pay attention. I even got moved to the front of the room in French class. Madam said some long sentence that I only barely caught. She was really mad at me. She said something about having the smarts but not being able to do the work.

If only I could explain to her what was going on in my head she could at least try to understand my condition.

Finally 3:10 arrived and Tanya and I met in the gym. Slowly students began to arrive and my stomach got tighter and tighter. I looked at Tanya and prayed that she felt at least a little more comfortable in front of a group.

Tanya looked at me sympathetically, then brushed her hand over my shoulder. It was a simple reassuring touch but it made me feel a whole lot better.

At exactly 3:15 we began the first official meeting of Match Made before Heaven.

"Welcome everyone!" Just as Tanya began Mr. French slipped in through the side doors and gave us a nod and a smile.

"Well, as you know, we've been working on getting this club organized for a while now. I think most of you know me, but in case you don't, my name is Tanya Miller and I'm in class 8B. We are really excited about starting this new club and thank you for volunteering to be the first participants ever!

"We have made arrangements to have our first visit to the seniors' residence this Thursday from 5:00 to 6:30 p.m. It will be an introductory meeting and a party. You will be introduced to your partner and we'll have a few things to say and then it'll be time to socialize and enjoy yourselves.

"At that time you will need to make arrangements with your partner for your next visit. That visit will take place sometime during the following week whenever it's convenient for both of you. Visits can be for an hour or you can arrange to go for two half-hours." Tanya took a deep breath and carried on. She sounded as if she'd been speaking in front of a group for *years!*

"In a moment we will give you the names of your partners and a brief biography of them. You can review your cards and let us know if you have any questions. What I'd like to do now is introduce you to the vice-president of our club, Shelagh Howard. Shelagh?"

Tanya motioned to me with a wave of her hand and stepped back. Her natural manner in front of a group only made it more difficult for me as I stepped forward to begin.

"Thank you, Tanya. Well, some of you will know me from class but for those of you who don't, my name is Shelagh Howard, I'm in 8A and I'm helping Tanya out. I'm really excited about this club and if you have any questions at any time I'd be happy to ask them . . . I mean *answer* them." What a stupid mistake! As I looked up everyone was giggling and I realized it wasn't such a big deal.

We'd practised this whole thing yesterday and once I started it wasn't as bad as I thought it'd be (even with the mistake). Next it was my job to introduce Mr. French as our teacher sponsor.

"Hecch, hecch!" I cleared my throat and smiled what I imagined to be a model-like smile. I stood tall (all five feet three inches of me) and I composed myself the way I thought I should. If I felt nervous before, it was nothing compared with how I felt now.

"The third member of our organizing team is our teacher sponsor. I know you'll all be happy to hear that Mr. French has agreed to join our club. Mr. French?"

The group smiled at each other and gave a small round of applause as Mr. French walked to the front of the gym.

"Thanks, Shelagh and Tanya. Well, guys and girls, I'm really excited for all of you. These two have been working really hard on your behalf and I expect it to be a very successful endeavour. From looking around at you folks I can see a very positive and energetic group and wish all of you great success. Good luck!"

Everyone clapped loudly at this because it truly was a great group and they were very enthusiastic.

"Okay, next on the agenda is to give out the names of your partners." Tanya had everyone's attention again.

Tanya and I wandered through the group finding the students whose names were on our cards. As we passed them out we heard little giggles of excitement and pleasure and questions about what was on the cards.

"What's crawchet?" One girl asked as her eyebrows furrowed in the middle of her forehead.

I glanced over her shoulder and saw the word *crochet* written on her card. I leaned in with a smile and said, "I think it's pronounced *cro-shay*." She glanced up, smiled back and said, "Oh! I've heard of that!"

"Oh, my gawd!" someone exclaimed. "My grandpa's only sixty-five and this guy is ninety-two!"

I was pleased already. It was great to see a reaction even if it was shock.

"Okay, everyone needs to look over their cards and see what kind of information is on them. One thing you'll need to do before Thursday is write one of these about yourself to give to your partner. Any questions?"

The group looked around at each other and grinned shyly. No one put up a hand. I was pretty sure they'd be asking questions later.

"Okay, the final thing we wanted to do was brainstorm some ideas of what we can do with our partners during these visits. An hour might not seem very long, but if the conversation isn't going very well it's good to have a backup plan." Once again Tanya sounded like a pro.

We had borrowed some markers and large sheets of paper from the art room and it was now my job to write down the suggestions.

By the end of the brainstorming session we had about twenty activities and other ideas of things to do with our partners. Everything from reading aloud to those seniors who'd lost their sight to going for a walk around the block.

There was a really wonderful feeling as the students made their way out of the gym. Tanya and I got a quick glimpse of one another and we both flashed great big grins. We were then stopped by students with questions as everyone mingled out.

All of a sudden there was a boy in front of me. I thought his name was Tom Braite, as I'd handed him his card, but I couldn't say for sure. He was in 8B and had kind of kept to himself last year. He paused as if he was going to say something, but he just smiled. He brushed past me and I felt a warm sensation on my arm. I turned around and wondered where the energy had come from. I'd never even noticed him before, but suddenly his dirty blond hair and piercing blue eyes were extremely noticeable!

Had he meant to say something or was he just on his way out the door?

I walked in a bit of a daze towards Tanya, who was taking down the poster paper. I was tempted to ask her if she knew him, but decided to wait until Thursday night to see if the sensation was all in my imagination.

Chapter 7

Wednesday night a totally disastrous thing happened. I was sitting in my room at my desk trying desperately to concentrate on some homework. My mind was in a wandering mood and I was pretty sure that no matter how many bricks I tried to lay on my daydreams they would not cease!

How could anyone expect me to do homework? Our introduction party was the next night, Mr. French would be there and so would Tom, Tom Braite (I did a little asking and found out that *was* his name), and I would also finally get to meet Dorothy. With all this excitement my mind was reeling through the possible scenarios of the party.

Then I recieved an unexpected phone call. I could never have guessed that it would blow all of my plans out of control.

"Shelagh! It's for you. It's Mom!" Jane yelled to me from the living room downstairs.

"Okay!" I hollered and ran into Dad's room to get the phone. I often dreaded talking to Mom but if I'd had any idea of what was about to happen I would never even have agreed to take the call.

As I picked up the receiver in Dad's room I told Jane that I had it and I settled onto Dad's bed with my head on the pillow and the phone at my ear.

"Hi, Mom. How's it going?"

"Good, Shelagh. How are you?"

"Oh, I'm pretty good. Not much going on . . . you know what it's like." Telling Mom about what was happening at school was a whole different story than telling Dad. And I had no intention of sharing anything with her. Well, at least as little as possible.

"So tomorrow night, you, me, Brad, dinner. How's it sound?"

"Pardon? Mom? Tomorrow night? Who's Brad?"

"Well, I'm sure I told you all about him. He wants to meet you. He's my new boss. I got a great new job. It's just fabulous and, well, you might as well know Brad's more than my boss."

"Well, Mom, you see there's this thing at school that I'm doing and our first event is tomorrow night. So actually . . ." I paused to think, "I can't go."

I'd never said no to Mom before. Jane and Jake and I had always had separate visits with Mom and she had decided it was now my turn. I was getting scared. What if she made me go? What if she didn't understand how much the club meant to me? My head started spinning as I thought of the terrible consequences.

"Well, Shelagh, I'm real sorry but you don't really have a choice here. That's what we agreed. I need you here with me for dinner and we've already made the arrangements. So I'll send Brad by to get you around 5:30. How's that sound then?"

Her question obviously had nothing to do with my saying no. The only answer she was looking for was, "Yeah, sure, Mom. That sounds great!"

"Uh . . . Mom. I think I need to explain something here. I've gotten involved in something at school. It's the most exciting thing I've ever done. It's so cool and there are all kinds of kids involved and well . . . it's just the best! And . . ."

She cut me off. "That's great, hon! I'd love to hear all about it tomorrow night. We'll have lots of time to catch up then. See you tomorrow!" And with that she hung up.

I could scream!

What was I going to do?

She made me so angry. How could she just *tell* me what to do? She hadn't even listened to what I said. No wonder I wasn't going to tell her about the club in the first place. I *knew* she wouldn't understand.

As I walked back to my room I noticed my fists were clenched. Suddenly I was aware that something breakable nearby might become broken.

How could my mom do this?

My mom had made her share of mistakes in her life and I tried not to hold it against her. But this was so typical of her. One time she showed up without notice, announcing that she had come to take me to a movie. But it was Jake's birthday and we were having a party. Dad had even invited her and never heard back. When she arrived at the door, she seemed to have no idea.

Now, for once, I actually had something exciting going on in *my* life. Something that I had helped organize and plan and was truly looking forward to. And then Mom shows up with her amazing ability to jump right in and ruin it all.

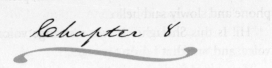

I had to think and I had to think fast. My brain was now in high gear. I hadn't been able to concentrate earlier on my homework but suddenly I was more focused than ever before. I needed to find a solution to tomorrow night's conflict.

I could just not come home. I could go straight to Tanya's and the retirement home and not be here when *Brad* came to get me. Or I could get Dad to call Mom. But he wouldn't be home until at least ten tonight. I could get Jane to go in my place. Why hadn't Mom just asked *her* in the first place? I could call her back and try to make her listen. Oh, God! What was I going to do?

Just then the phone rang again. I jumped at the sound of it. Jane must have answered it downstairs.

I kept walking slowly back towards my bedroom, head down, feeling low, when Jane yelled up that the phone was for me again.

I walked back towards my dad's room, picked up the phone and slowly said hello.

"Hi! Is this Shelagh?" It was a strange voice, a boy's voice, and one that I didn't recognize.

"Yes, this is Shelagh. Who's this?"

"It's Tom. I mean I'm Tom. Tom Braite. I don't think you actually know who I am but I'm in the club and we kind of met the other day at the meeting."

"Oh, hi, Tom. Yeah, I know who you are. I thought you might have had a question for me but then it turned out that you didn't." I smiled enough that he might have been able to hear it through the phone.

"Yeah, well, actually I did. I was going to ask you but then all of a sudden I just lost my nerve. It's silly, really, because it's not a big thing. I don't know quite what happened but I just kept walking instead of stopping to chat."

"That's okay!" Again another big smile. "So do you still have the question?"

"Oh, ha! Yah, I do. Umm, I was just wondering if you'd like us to bring something for the party. It's kind of embarrassing but my mom kept asking me if there was something we should be bringing, like cookies or something. And now that it's the night before, she wants to know if she should be helping me bake." He kind of chuckled at the end and I thought he sounded really sweet.

"Well, umm. We hadn't really talked about it. Tanya was just going to pick up some chips. It sounds like a great idea, though, and I'm sure that everyone would appreciate something home-baked. It's up to you really. Tell your mom it's a great idea. I wish we'd thought of it earlier."

"Okay. I'll see how eager she really is on baking so I don't have to do all the work. Well, I just wanted to ask you that so I guess I'll see you tomorrow night. That is if I don't pass you in the halls tomorrow."

Oh, the torture of it all. Tom was calling *me* and I wasn't even going to be there.

"Oh, yeah. That sounds great, but I'm afraid I might not be able to go."

"What do you mean? You guys put this whole thing together. You *have* to go!"

"I know. It's kind of hard to explain."

"I've got time."

"Oh, ha!" I laughed nervously. "Well, it's a long story and I'm not really sure what I'm going to do about it. I need to think of a solution right now. But thanks anyway."

"Okay, well, good luck. I really hope to see you there."

"Thanks. I really hope to be there!"

"Bye!"

"Bye."

Jane pushed her head into Dad's room just as I put the phone back down. She had teasing eyes.

"Who was *thaa-at?!*" Jane smiled at me wickedly. She was ready to taunt.

I thought tears just might come to my eyes if I didn't resist them with everything I had. The guy who made my arm go numb when he walked by PHONED me! And he had called at the exact moment that I was trying to figure out how to get my demanding mother out of my life. Well, for one night anyway.

Jane suddenly stopped the teasing stare, came into the room and sat quietly on Dad's bed.

"What's up?" She must have seen the tears brewing in the corners of my eyes. She waited for me to answer. She was patient and for the first time ever I realized I might actually be able to talk to her.

"Well, tomorrow night is our big night at the centre. It's the first meeting where everyone will be paired up and we've been planning it for weeks. Then Mom calls and *tells* me that I'll be going out for dinner with her and *Brad* tomorrow night."

"Who's *Brad?*" Jane had never heard his name either.

"EXACTLY! Who's *Brad?!!* Her boss and boyfriend I guess."

"Ha!" Jane laughed at this, a knowing laugh that said, "Not surprised. That's Mom for you!"

"Yeah, I know. I told her I was busy but she didn't even listen. She just spoke over top of what I was saying and said 'See you tomorrow!'

"Oh, yeah . . . and then TOM phoned me. That was him just now." I didn't even bother to explain who he was. I said it as though Jane should know exactly what all this meant.

"And who's Tom . . . ?"

"Well, he's in the club and he's really cute and he seems really nice and he CALLED me!" Now I was sounding really pathetic.

"Oooooh, smoochy smoochy and you're going to miss the party. I get it!" She was making fun but at the same time she sounded as though she understood my problem. "Well, you've got yourself quite a situation here. I feel for you, I really do." Jane smiled at me, leaned over and gave me a warm lingering hug.

Despite her attempt at kindness she was not going to solve my problem. I hugged her back, grateful for our little talk, and I fell back onto Dad's bed as she left.

After a lot of careful thinking I came up with a plan. It wasn't very smart or brave and maybe a little bit cowardly but I couldn't help it. I decided it was my only hope.

I sat down and wrote a letter to Betty. It explained in great detail what the situation was, what my solution was and how I was unfortunately using her to deflect the trouble. I begged her to tell Brad, when he arrived tomorrow, that I wasn't able to go with him.

It was a terrible burden to put on Betty, but I thought she might understand. I decided to leave the letter in our mailbox where she would find it later in the afternoon. By then I'd be at the retirement home getting set up and praying to God that the whole world didn't come crashing down when Brad showed up.

Chapter 9

I had the most restless sleep I'd ever had. I woke up, had a shower, packed my knapsack and left with only a quick goodbye to Betty. I usually sat down for breakfast and discussed my day with her. She was sure to know something was wrong but I couldn't bear to face her.

I put the letter in the mailbox as I left and slowly walked towards the bus stop at the end of my street. It would take a lot of energy and a lot of guts to ignore what I had just done and enjoy the day for what it should have been. I was pretty determined to put it out of my mind and look forward to this evening.

Tanya and I had worked hard for tonight and we deserved to get excited as the day went on instead of dreading it.

I succeeded fairly well for most of the day. I smiled at my friends and other club members in the hall as I passed them between classes. I dreamily went from class to class trying not to think of the possibility of impending doom.

I found myself outside of math class, my last period of the day. Mr. French. A relief. Maybe he'd take my mind off my worries.

I walked in, books in hand, and realized that Mr. French was trying to get my attention.

"Shelagh, the office just buzzed—they want you down there a.s.a.p." He looked worried for me.

Oh, God! What was happening? Betty wouldn't have called Dad would she? I looked at my watch and realized she could have opened the letter by now.

As I walked towards the office my hands began to sweat. Who would be waiting for me—my mom, my dad, Betty? What kind of trouble was I in?

My heart was pounding as I rounded the corner.

When I spotted Betty I sighed with a brief feeling of relief but the look on her face was solid as a rock—I had no idea if I was in serious trouble or if I was going to be patted on the back.

"You, young lady, have a job to do!"

"I guess you got my note." It was more a statement than a question.

"Of course I did. Why do you think I'm here?" She paused for effect, still leaving me wondering. "Shelagh, I was livid when I received your note. Half at you for leaving me to deal with this problem and half at your mother for putting you in this situation. You are thirteen years old now. And unfortunately, from what I know of your mother, you are going to be dealing with these kinds of situations for the rest of your life." Betty looked at me with compassion, concern and a touch of that anger that had flared up earlier.

"I didn't know what to do. You know how much tonight means to me and I really tried to solve this another way. I thought and thought and thought. I nearly drove myself crazy last night. I even told Jane, but she didn't volunteer any bright answers. It was the only thing I could think of and I knew you'd understand." I looked at her with pleading eyes.

"Well, as much as I do understand how this must have distressed you, I really wish you'd come and talked to me about it last night. Why didn't you tell me then? I was downstairs helping Jake with his exercises when your mom called and by the time the phone rang the second time I was finished putting him to bed. I expected more from you this time, Shelagh."

Now I was disappointed in myself. I knew Betty was right and I knew deep down that I was being cowardly. It was time to apologize to Betty and then figure out what to do.

"Betty, I'm really sorry. You're right. I don't know why I didn't talk to you last night. I guess I was scared. I was so overwhelmed by everything that I couldn't think straight. Thank you for not hating me."

"Of course I don't hate you. But we do have some things to take care of and the sooner the better for everyone. First things first: *you* are going to phone your mother. You are going to explain to her that you have a prior commitment that cannot be broken. And you will explain to her that you are sorry you weren't able to explain this last night but that is where you will be tonight!"

"Betty?! Are you sure?" I was shocked. Happy but shocked.

"I only needed a few minutes to know that this was the only answer. And, yes, I am sure. Now where is there a phone that we can use?"

I directed her around the corner to the pay phone for students and she handed me a quarter.

"Dial."

I'd never seen her look so serious and yet so sure of herself. I'm glad that she explained how she was half mad at me and half mad at my mom. Until Betty said it I didn't realize how wrong it was for my mom to bully me into going to dinner with her tonight. I knew *I* was angry, but for Betty to get fired up enough to come all the way down here and make me stand up for myself was really incredible.

I carefully dialled Mom's number and realized I was going to get her machine. I hung up and lost the quarter.

"I need to think first. It was the machine." I paused and thought out my message while I hoped and prayed I'd get the machine again.

"You've reached 555-2367. Please leave a message and I'll be happy to return your call." Beeeep . . .

"Hi, Mom. It's Shelagh. I'm very sorry to tell you this but I will not be home when Brad comes to get me this evening. I tried to explain last night. I have a prior commitment that I cannot miss. I hope you understand how important this is to me. I really wish I'd been able to make this clear when I talked to you last night. I will talk to you later . . . Okay . . . Bye."

I hung up and Betty gave me a great big hug. I felt an enormous sense of relief.

"Now doesn't that feel better? Even if it was her machine . . ." Betty paused and looked straight into my eyes. I felt like I'd made such a silly mistake and to get Betty involved had made it worse.

"My dear. I understand why you wrote the note to me. I'm grateful that you trust me enough to help you. But you must remember in the future that you need to do what is right by you. You have worked hard on this club and you deserve to be there tonight. It's going to be tough and a lot of kids are going to be really nervous, including you. But you and Tanya have organized a wonderful event and it will lead to a very rewarding year. Your mother certainly shouldn't make you miss it. If by chance your mother doesn't get the message I will be home to greet Brad and send him on his way." She smiled now and I couldn't think of the words to thank her enough.

"Betty, thank you. Thank you for coming. Thank you for everything." This time I hugged *her*.

"All right then. You need to get back to class and I have to pick up Jake. Good luck. Call me from the centre when you're finished. I'll send your dad if he's home." Another smile and she was down the stairs and out the door.

Chapter 10

Tanya and I walked to her house after school. I had a new bounce in my step after seeing Betty. I was now free to enjoy the evening and to finally get excited about our big night.

We entered through the back door of the centre, which was the front door to Tanya's house. Two of Tanya's brothers came in at the same time. They were both older than us and looked in the mood to tease.

"You here with your goodie-goodie friend to start the oldies club?" the tallest one said in a taunting voice.

"Bug off, Calvin!" She turned to me. "These are my brothers. Don't bother saying hi!"

I kind of smiled out of embarrassment and followed Tanya into the front hall.

"Have fun having your tea and cookies!! Don't forget the prune juice!!" one of them yelled after us.

Tanya grabbed my arm and started walking faster through a long hall and into another room. She pushed open a door and all of a sudden there was a bright room full of furniture, paintings and beautiful stained-glass lamps.

Tanya turned to look at me. "Sorry, my brothers are morons. They have no idea how to behave. It's like they just got out of kindergarten and are still learning their manners."

"It's okay. I luckily don't have to go through that because my brother is younger and my sister, who's older, just ignores me most the time." I smiled and began to look around.

"Well, this is it. What do you think?"

"It's great! It'll be perfect for tonight. Where's all the stuff?"

"Oh, I put it under here." Tanya walked around behind a counter and opened a cupboard. She pulled out the balloons, streamers, cups, plates and signs we'd gotten earlier.

I looked around and noticed two old men and an old woman sitting in reading chairs. One was listening to a Walkman that I could hear from where I was standing, and the other two were just sitting there kind of staring off into the distance.

Out of the blue I started to giggle. It was the kind that

bubbles up from inside and you have no control over. I couldn't even say what made me start laughing but I was afraid once I started I wouldn't be able to stop. I think it was a combination of nerves, excitement and seeing the place I'd been thinking about for weeks.

Tanya gave me a funny grin wondering what had started me off and I had to turn away towards a wall to try to compose myself. Of all the times to have a giggle-fit I wasn't expecting it to be here and now.

I finally pulled myself together so that I could help Tanya get set up. We started blowing up balloons, taping up streamers. Tanya took care of the food table and set out the bags of chips and other snacks.

The more we did, it seemed the faster time went by. I started to worry about getting everything done by five.

Just then an older woman, shorter than me and very well dressed with makeup and hair done just perfectly, entered the room. She was pushing a walker in front of her but managed a very easy-looking stride. There was something almost regal about her and yet approachable at the same time. I was drawn to her appearance and realized I was staring.

She wore a thin pink cardigan, which looked hand-knit, and a long thick jean skirt, which looked very hip on this cool old lady. Her hair was short, grey and styled so that it had a little flair to it.

I wondered to myself what was so intriguing about her and I started to tell myself I'd better stop staring when I realized she was heading straight towards me.

"I'm Dorothy," she said as she gave me a beautiful warm smile.

"Oh! Hi! I'm Shelagh." I was stunned. This woman was my partner. I was so overwhelmed, relieved and happy.

She leaned forward to touch my hand. It wasn't a shake so much as a grasp. We were holding hands. Her knuckles were small and bent. Her skin was pulled tightly over her bones but she had a firm grip and a warm hand.

"I know, I know. Tanya told me all about you. It's a pleasure to finally meet you, dear."

She worked her way around her walker in order to sit on the seat that made up part of the walker. I edged her around and helped her find her place. She seemed grateful, patted my hand and then slowly let go.

I felt lost for the briefest moment as her warm hand fell from mine. I had been connected somehow to her. Something had passed between us.

Dorothy smiled at me again and said, "Now what exactly do you girls need help with? I was the first one done upstairs so I thought I'd better mosey on down and give you a hand. You should see them up there. You'd think the Queen was coming for tea! They're primping, trying to look young and beautiful again."

I smiled. "Hmmm, could you give me some advice about where to put the rest of the balloons?"

"Let me see," she took a quick glance around the room. "You've done an excellent job so far. How about a couple by the front door where the students will come in and then the rest on the backs of the chairs."

Dorothy and I spent the next twenty minutes putting up balloons and deciding what combinations would work best. It may seem like a pretty normal thing to do but I was having fun.

I looked up as Tom and the two other boys came in the front door of the common room from the main hall. Tom gave me a little nod and a wave. I smiled, waved back and felt a flush of warmth in my cheeks. I turned to tie the final ribbon onto the back of the chair in front of me. Dorothy had a large knowing grin and I was afraid to guess what was going on in her mind.

"Now he's a handsome young man, isn't he? Is he your beau?" Dorothy was smiling at me and you could tell she was loving every minute of it.

I was pretty sure what she meant but I wasn't ready to admit it. I played dumb. *"Beau?"*

"You know . . . your boyfriend, your right-hand man, your partner in crime, your *beau*." She paused to think.

"I guess it's an old word, isn't it? Well, there is a certain chemistry between you two. I can sense it from here." She looked as though she might bubble over with joy.

My mouth must have been agape because she started laughing out loud when she turned to look at me. I had small personal, private, secret feelings for Tom, which even I hadn't completely acknowledged, and here she was saying she could feel the chemistry between us across a large room. Could she read my mind? Maybe Dorothy had supernatural powers. There were many possible reasons for what she'd said but her sensing chemistry between us couldn't possibly be one of them. Could it?

Slowly all the students filed in as they were dropped off by parents and friends' parents. And two by two the seniors also came down the hall from the elevator into the common room and found seats. At 5:07 Mr. French arrived with a grocery bag full of pop and chips.

Everyone was being very polite and having quiet little conversations when Tanya decided to begin.

"Okay, everyone, may I have your attention please?" She waited for everyone to quiet down.

"First of all I'd like to welcome all of you to our centre this evening. It is a great pleasure for the club members to be here and to finally get the chance to meet you." She paused again to see that everyone was paying attention.

"The first part of our evening will be spent introducing each student to his or her partner. You'll then have a chance to get to know each other and finally we'll have some fun activities!"

Slowly, one by one, Tanya read off the names of the students and their corresponding partner. They came to the front of the room, said hello to each other and paired off. As the last pair was seated, Dorothy waved me over to where she had been waiting and patted the seat beside her.

I had it all planned—what I was going to tell her about my life and what questions I would ask about hers.

"So, you go first. I want to know everything. Your family, your friends, your dreams, your fears." She smiled and I thought to myself, Yes, I could probably sit here all night and tell her every single thought that entered my head. The quiet way she was willing to listen unconditionally made me want to blurt everything out. So I took a deep breath, looked over the cue card I'd made to give her and began.

"I live with my older sister, Jane, my younger brother, Jake, and my dad. We also have a housekeeper or nurse and her name is Betty. My brother has cerebral palsy, so she helps look after him. My mom doesn't live with us and to tell you the truth I'm a little afraid of the wrath that she may lay upon me shortly."

I stopped. This was not on my card. It certainly wasn't what I had planned to say.

Dorothy looked inquisitive. She raised her eyebrows ever so slightly, encouraging me to continue.

And so I did.

The words came tumbling out. I told her everything—from my mom leaving us, our sporadic visits, my growing dislike for her to the letter I'd written to Betty and the subsequent phonecall to my mom.

As I spoke I realized that if Mom hadn't gotten the message Brad could very well be standing on our front porch right now, waiting for someone to answer the door. I kind of smiled at the thought of Betty giving him a good tongue-lashing.

Dorothy frowned and started to ask some more specific questions. I answered freely, happy to be getting the whole situation off my chest.

She was so easy to talk to. I'd never felt like spilling the beans to anyone like this before. She was sympathetic without being condescending.

She seemed to accept every word I said as the truth. She was completely supportive.

As Tanya and I were cleaning up, I thought back to the wonder of the evening. It had been the most amazing success. While I was confessing my life story to Dorothy, all the other pairs were happily chatting away. And as the evening wore on, Tanya and I held a quick game show. We played "How Well Do You Know Your Partner?" We had a series of questions for each pair. They knew so much about each other Tanya and I were overwhelmed—and grateful that we'd gotten extra prizes just in case.

Before Mr. French left he had come to see us and was full of praise. He'd had the chance to meet some of the seniors and said he was very impressed with the whole thing. Of course I was beaming the whole while he was speaking and had to pull myself down from the clouds when he was done.

Finally the time came to call home to see who was going to come and get me. I also wanted to know whether or not Mom had gotten my message. Tanya led me to the main phone in the common room and I slowly dialled my number.

"Hello?" It was Jane.

"Hi! It's me. Is Dad home yet?"

"Oh, boy! Do I have a story for you." She sounded strange—not angry—and seemingly happy to hear my voice. "Yeah, he's here. Do you want to talk to him? It might not be the best idea. He's pretty angry. I think I should just send him over to get you."

"Oh, God! What happened? Why's Dad mad? Did Betty tell him?"

"Don't worry about it. I'll tell you everything when you get home. Oh and by the way . . . he's not mad at you. He's mad at me!"

"Oh? Now I'm curious." What *was* going on?

"Yeah, I'll tell you everything as soon as you get here."

"Okay. Thanks, Jane."

"No problem. Bye."

"Bye."

She sounded somewhat amused by the whole thing, even at the fact that Dad was angry. As I waited for him by the doors of the common room I thought about my talk with Jane last night. I heard the same thing in her voice tonight. I felt like she really wanted to tell me what happened and she wanted to *talk* to me. Although I pretended not to care about my older sister who just ignored me most of the time, I now knew what it meant to be wanted by her and truthfully it felt good.

Dad picked me up a while later with an angry attitude. He barely spoke to me as I got into the car. He kind of grunted and mumbled something about "that sister of yours . . ." Now I was even more curious. How had Jane become involved?

A few minutes into the drive he finally asked me how my evening had gone, but it seemed to be with great reluctance that he spoke to me at all. Maybe the quiet of the car was too much for him.

At first I was too petrified to answer. I hadn't seen Dad this mad in a long time. Jane had seemed almost gleeful and yet Dad was furious. What *had* happened tonight?

Since I was going to have to wait anyway and I really wanted to tell Dad how it had all gone, I began to go over, in great detail, the entire evening. Dad gradually warmed up and listened. He even asked questions and nodded and smiled here and there. As I reviewed the night, talking about Tanya and Dorothy (I left out Tom, for now), I got lost in my own dream world. I loved explaining it all to him but when we pulled into the drive my dream came to a sudden halt. Dad simply said Jane had done something very wrong.

Chapter 11

Jane, with a huge grin on her face, was waiting for me in the living room. She told me to put down my stuff and have a seat on the couch. I did so but her ear-to-ear smile couldn't stop me from wondering *what* was going on.

"So," she began, "Betty told me how you tried to call Mom today and ended up leaving a message." Jane was still smiling. She looked over my shoulder suspiciously, waiting for Dad to come through the living-room door.

"Yeah . . . ?!" I nodded questioningly.

"And, well, the thing is, Mom didn't get the message."

"Yeah, well, I kind of figured that much out. So what happened?" Now I frowned. What did she find so funny that Dad was so upset about?

"Okay, so Brad shows up." She looked at me in anticipation.

"Uhun . . ." I nodded again.

Just then Dad walked into the living room.

He shook his head. "This is not happening here." He looked directly at Jane. "If you are going to relay this story to Shelagh it is going to be in one of your bedrooms. I'm not going to sit here and listen to this nonsense again." He looked mad but really he was much calmer than he'd been earlier.

Jane grabbed my hand and pulled me upstairs, around the corner and into the hallway. She threw open her door and flopped on her bed. She had the best duvet in the world. She'd asked for it last year for Christmas as her only present because they're really expensive. You could sink right into it and never come out.

I'd never actually been in Jane's room while she was home. I'd only ever been in here while I *knew* she was out. This time I lay on the bed and snuggled in. Jane sat cross-legged beside me and jumped right back into her story about Brad knocking on the front door.

"So he knocked on the door and before I could say anything, he began, 'Now isn't this lovely? You must be Shelagh. Your mom has told me an awful lot about you. I'm glad *you* answered the door. I wouldn't have wanted to have to see your dad right away or have to ask for you. So are you ready to go?' I looked at him stunned and had a terrible but wonderful little thought. I told him I'd be right back and went to let Betty know that Brad had shown up and so I was going to go in your place." She paused to see my reaction so far.

"Oh . . . thanks . . . I guess." I was grateful she'd taken my place but I was worried about her motives.

"No, no, it get's better. I kind of decided to play along with him because he hadn't even given me the chance to speak. He may have been a little nervous but still he could have started with a 'hello' or something!"

"Do you mean he still thought you were me?" I was aghast.

"Yup! So as we got into the car, I'm thinking to myself, How can I make the best out of a bad situation? I didn't want to be totally mean but I did want to have a little fun."

Jane continued with glee. "As we chatted in the car *my* name came up. I explained that *Jane* was kind of a pain in the butt, that she wasn't very friendly and it was a good thing she didn't answer the door. He asked me why and I said something like, 'Oh, you don't want to know.'

"Now this is the best part. *He* says, 'Yeah, I know. I got that impression from your mom.' I said, 'Oh, really? What do you mean?' And he said, 'Well I probably shouldn't say anything but . . . your mom said she would put me off meeting your sister until absolutely necessary. Your mom doesn't want to scare me off.' Can you believe it?!?!"

Jane burst out laughing. She was almost totally out of control in fits of hysterical laughter. She even had tears streaming down her face.

I propped myself up and stared right at her with my mouth wide open. I couldn't believe it! What had she done? She'd continued with the joke that she was me and then it had been thrown back in her face. Somehow she still thought this was funny!

She finally stopped laughing and continued.

"So anyway," she went on, "it gets even better. We arrive at the restaurant and Mom is already there waiting at the table. She looked really surprised to see me and said, '*Jane*, what are *you* doing here?'

"The look on Brad's face was priceless. He looked completely distraught and ashamed and yet he couldn't even let on to Mom that anything was wrong. It was the best! Mom seemed okay with it all when I explained that you were busy and had left a message. I was sure to give Brad a good wink and a lovely smile and then we sat down to a pretty quick meal!"

"Jane! Oh, my God. You never said anything?"

"Nope! And Mom will likely never know. If Brad feels guilty enough for talking badly about me to my face he will never tell her what happened."

That was true. But it seemed so dishonest.

"And just think how much fun it will be. Every visit we have with them I'll be able to simply smile and very likely drive Brad completely mad!"

"Jane, you are totally amazing!" I finally allowed myself a smile.

She was still grinning ear to ear. She was loving every minute of putting Brad into a desperate and ongoing situation.

I couldn't believe she'd pulled that off. I would never have had the nerve to even pretend for a moment that I was someone else. What must Brad think of her now!

I almost wished it had affected Mom. That was an evil thought. But really Brad was relatively innocent in this whole thing. His only crime was that he was hanging out with Mom. I guess that's how Jane gets back at her.

Jane continued, "So that's why Dad was so mad. He was not impressed with me or my story when I told him."

I had to take all this in. *I* wasn't in trouble, likely wouldn't get into trouble and I'd had one of the best nights of my life. Well, my life so far.

"Jane, I can't believe you did all that. Weren't you nervous he might say something?"

"Well, at first I just thought it'd be a funny joke and I'd tell him in the car but he kept making it worse by saying that stuff about me!" Jane screwed up her face into a hilarious contortion.

Now I laughed and so did she. As I rolled over on the bed I felt evil again for enjoying this so much. What Jane had done was wrong, that's what Dad would say, but truthfully I loved it! Part of it was that she'd kind of saved my butt in Mom's eyes by going at all. The other part was that we were sitting on her bed together, laughing our heads off about something so devious and funny.

We sat there for a long time. We talked and we laughed some more. I even told her about my night at the centre. I kept it short. I knew she wasn't *that* interested. It turns out that she goes to school with one of Tanya's brothers. I never knew that before.

Eventually Dad knocked on the door and said it was time we stopped giggling and went to bed. I wondered for a moment if, despite all this nonsense, it made him happy to see Jane and me talking and having a good time. It had been a long time coming and I was pretty sure he was all too aware of that.

I made Jane promise me that on our next visit with Mom we would go together. She said, "You got it!" And for once in a long while I felt my life was complete.

As I got into bed and turned on my bedside light, Dad came in.

"You need to know, young lady, that what Jane did tonight was wrong." He frowned but the anger was gone.

"I know that, Dad. I never had any intention of any of that happening when I told Mom I couldn't go."

"I know you didn't, but I just don't want her setting a bad example for you."

Poor Jane. She was getting knocked by both Mom and Dad for being a terrible person.

"Dad, I know right from wrong."

"Okay, hon. I just needed to clarify that. Have a good sleep."

As I lay in bed I tried to put thoughts of Brad and Mom and Jane and Dad out of my head. Instead I relived my evening: my first visit with Dorothy and the first meeting of all the volunteers with their partners. I tried to fall asleep but was kept awake by the images of our evening—from decorating, to talking, to playing our quiz game. What was left in my mind as I finally fell asleep was that Match Made before Heaven was now truly an official club.

Chapter 12

At school the next morning I felt very contented and balanced. I'd heard about this feeling before, when I read a picture book about eastern religions. I read about meditation and feeling nothingness and feeling everything all at once. That was how I felt this morning.

At the same time, I desperately wanted to see Tom. I wasn't sure why but we hadn't really had the chance to talk last night and I wanted to see how it had been with his partner. I wanted to ask Tom what his partner was like, how old he was and how their conversation had gone.

There was another reason I wanted to see him. Of all the things that were going well in my life, with the club and my family, I still felt that having Tom as a friend would make it that much better.

I was at school earlier than usual because Dad said he'd drop me off. I was grateful for the time alone. I sat on the swings in the little kids' area for awhile, just thinking, dreaming and enjoying that rare feeling of pure happiness.

I looked at my watch and realized the other kids probably wouldn't show up for another ten or fifteen minutes. As I looked up, slowly kicking the ground to get me going, I saw him walking straight towards me. This must be part of my daydream. I shook my head to clear it.

His image didn't go away.

"Hey, Shelagh! Why are you here so early?"

It was Tom.

"Hi. Oh . . . my dad was going into work later than normal so he dropped me off. Why are you here?"

"I live across the street!"

"Oh!" My head was spinning for some reason. I was getting that tickly feeling in my arms again. He lived across the street! I wondered suddenly if he'd seen me from his house. Had he seen me with my head dropped back, swinging wildly back and forth? Had he wanted to tell me I might hurt myself? Had he wanted to just see me and talk?

"Yeah, so I thought I'd come over and chat!"

Unbelievable!

"Oh, that's great! I'm glad you did." I didn't want to sound *too* interested. "So what'd you think of last night?

I didn't get a chance to see you before you left." I was so proud of how things had gone but I was still really curious to hear what an objective voice would have to say about it.

Tom sat down on the swing next to mine and gently began rocking back and forth.

"Shelagh, it was really amazing. You guys did such a good job of organizing it all. It was great."

"Thanks. So what was your partner like? I saw you talking with him but I couldn't see him very well."

"Well . . . his name is William. And he's seventy-four years old." He paused and looked unsure of whether to continue. "Um . . . I don't really know what else to say. I think he might be sick. You know with Alzheimer's or something? He asked me the same questions a few times and seemed genuinely interested and surprised at my answer every time.

"He was very nice otherwise and it will still be interesting meeting with him. But I am a little afraid that he won't know who I am each time."

"Wow. That must be hard. But I'm sure he really appreciates having someone to talk to. Maybe you should ask Tanya if there is anything more you should know about him or anything specific you could do with him."

"Yeah, I will . . ."

The next fifteen minutes were a joy, a simple pleasure and a dream come true.

Slowly kids started arriving in the playground but we were oblivious to them. We talked about the club, about our families and ourselves. I told him the story about Jane and Brad and he found it as funny as Jane did.

When the bell went, I thought that I would give just about anything to stay out on those swings, swinging back and forth, slowly kicking the dirt and talking with Tom.

Tom grabbed my arm and my knapsack and we ran all the way into school, laughing and tripping most of the way in. We said goodbye, we smiled and then we went our separate ways towards our lockers.

My heart hurt. Was that possible? Maybe I was having a heart attack. Whoever heard of a thirteen-year-old having a heart attack? It was like a deep throbbing pain. My whole upper body ached.

As I walked down the hall, I realized that it also felt wonderful. How could that be? Tom was making me feel this way and I wasn't sure if I should be angry for the pain or grateful for the pleasure.

The day wore on and these feelings came and went. When I caught a glimpse of the back of his shirt, they came rushing back to me, almost making me dizzy. This was all very new to me and I was pretty sure it was a good thing, but my final judgement was still not in.

It was Friday afternoon. After all that had happened the last couple of nights I felt really ready for the weekend. As I finished getting my homework together I put it in my knapsack, closed my locker door, pushed my lock shut and turned sharply—directly into Tom.

"Hi!"

"Hi!"

"Sorry to bug you."

"No, it's okay!" I hoped my voice didn't sound too enthusiastic.

"You probably just want to get home but I was wondering if I could walk with you."

"Yeah, sure. It's kind of far. But if you don't mind I'd love the company." There it was again. That pain in my chest. It was like I knew that if he suddenly said he couldn't go, the pain might turn into some crushing force that would pin me to the ground.

"Well, if you're ready, let's go!" I looked closely at him and noticed that he had a very nice smile. I could get used to this!

Well, it was the dreamiest walk home ever. It was better than any daydream. It was the real thing.

When we got to my house I wasn't sure if I should invite him in. After all, he had walked me all the way home. I should at least offer him something to drink.

So I did. And Betty was very cool about the whole thing (well that is until he left). And just before he left we arranged to see our senior partners on Sunday at 2:00 p.m. We would double-check with them but if everything worked out we'd go together for our visit.

We said goodbye at the door and I thought how much I'd like to hug him. I didn't of course, but I realized how nice that might just be. Then he was gone down the street, kicking the leaves as he went.

Once again the pain was back.

"So, my dear. Who exactly is this *Tom* character?" Betty gave me a glowing, knowing smile and I smiled back.

"He's a friend from school. He's also a member of Match Made before Heaven. And . . . that's *all* I'm going to tell you." I grinned back at her, turned on my heels and headed for my room.

I lay on my bed, pain in chest, reliving every detail, every thought, every word we'd said. How my daydreams hadn't even compared to this feeling now! I chose my favourite song, put it in my CD player, put on my headphones and dreamed.

Chapter 13

Sunday afternoon rolled around. Dad was driving us to the centre, and coming back for us one hour later. Once we picked up Tom, my dad quizzed him and made even the short ride to the centre uncomfortable. Tom and I didn't say much to each other in the car.

We arrived at the centre and said bye to my dad. It felt awkward all of a sudden. I knew I still liked Tom but I didn't feel as relaxed as I had before. Was it because I hadn't stopped thinking about him since Friday night when he walked me home?

We entered the common room and there was Dorothy and Tom's partner, William. Tom and I kind of nodded to each other, smiled and went our separate ways to visit, talk, walk or play cards.

Now I was in my world with Dorothy. She still had that warm and welcome smile.

"Hi, dear. Come sit with me for awhile." She was already sitting on the couch and I wondered how long it had taken her to manoeuvre herself that way.

"Hi, Dorothy. How are you feeling today?" I sat next to her but facing her so that I could still see her well.

"Oh, I'm fine, dear. My heart feels pretty weak these days but I try to take it easy when I can. I had a visit yesterday from one of my grandchildren. She and her husband brought their two little ones so it was a busy visit. Oh, but I love to see them. They are sweet to me."

"That's wonderful. Do you just have the two great-grandchildren?"

"Yes, but I don't like to admit it. That means that I really *am* old." She smiled.

We talked for a little bit longer and then she said she'd like to go for a walk. I realized that I was able to completely immerse myself in conversation with her when we were together. As soon as we moved, I noticed Tom playing cards with William and my heart leapt into my throat.

I was determined not to think about him while I was enjoying my visit with Dorothy. We left the common room without her walker. She told me that as long as she had my arm to hold onto she'd be fine. I was a little worried about Dorothy's heart but she seemed to think it was okay. I prayed quietly to myself that our walk wouldn't be too much for her.

We went straight out the front door, slowly down the steps and onto the sidewalk. It was a beautiful fall day, clear and sunny. There were yellow, orange, red and brown leaves scattered across the sidewalk and the road. It was a perfect day for a walk.

Dorothy held my arm firmly and I tried my best to stay as steady as possible. She told me she wanted to go around the block and I was relieved when I noticed how short the block was. It wasn't that I didn't want to spend too much time with her, it was just that I was worried about getting back before it got dark!

I wanted to hear about her this time, so I asked her some questions. She was very willing to talk and I listened carefully. I tried to appear as she had to me: open-minded, ready to listen and non-judgemental.

"I imagine it's hard for kids like you to know what war was like. It destroyed us. It destroyed families, friends and neighbours. But at the same time it brought us together like nothing has since. It made us strong people in our hearts. And it made us know the value of life.

"That's when I met my husband, Frank. It was during the Second World War. I was a nurse and because I was so young and brave," she chuckled here, "I didn't really know any better. I volunteered to go to England to see what I could do to help.

"My parents were devastated. Their sons *had* to go but I didn't *have* to. They understood but they still didn't want to see me leave. I don't know that I would have done it again. I know that it has made me who I am today but what I saw will never leave the deep and dark parts of my memory.

"I met Frank about three days after I arrived in London. All the nurses were housed together in a dormitory-style building. We worked in local hospitals or we could be recruited to go farther into the field.

"Frank was our co-ordinator. He was responsible for sending the nurses to our posts and keeping track of where we were. He had been in the air force, but with a bad knee he'd sustained from an accident during training, he was left doing administrative work. He always managed to make the best of it. An amazing man. I don't imagine there's another one out there like him."

As she spoke I was reminded of my first talk with Tanya about Dorothy. Tanya had said that Dorothy's husband had recently passed away. That was why Dorothy was now at the centre. She seemed very capable of talking about him without getting too upset.

She continued, "Many men who were out of commission because of injuries became depressed and unable to serve anyone. But Frank was somehow able to go beyond that and he made whatever situation he was in the most challenging and rewarding he could. Once we started dating he would place me closer and closer to him, which was farther and farther from the fighting. He may have saved my life by doing that.

"He was British and once the war was over he agreed to start a new life with me in Canada. I had asked *him* to marry *me*. That was unheard of!" Dorothy roared with a full-bellowed laugh. I thought I saw tears in her eyes, but it might have been the shimmer from the bright sun.

Dorothy asked that we sit for awhile. We found a stone ledge that bordered someone's lawn. It was cold but we sat close as I continued to listen to her story.

"After the war, there were so many families separated, so many members lost. Those who'd died in battle. We were lucky and we knew it. Of my three brothers only one returned. My parents were destroyed by the news.

"When Frank and I came back to Canada we got married immediately. Frank managed to become like a son to my parents and he brought joy into their lives after such devastating losses. They were somewhat renewed when he was around, but of course they were never the same." Dorothy paused here and looked up into the sky. I wondered if she was saying a secret prayer for her parents who must have passed away ages ago.

Dorothy started again with an explanation of post-war life. "Small neat houses were built for those returning from the war. We became part of a wonderful little community of mostly young couples and our growing families.

"Frank was a little older than me, of course, but that was pretty common at the time. I never worked as a nurse again. I raised my children with my husband and we had a very full life.

"When we came to Canada he got into business. He was a very, very smart man and I truly believe he could have done anything he set his mind to. That is one of the many things I loved about him.

"Oh, how I miss him now." She sighed and there was a long pause. It was a simple, peaceful silence.

I tried to imagine how life would have been back then. The word *war* meant almost nothing to me. I pictured the Second World War as men fighting each other, wearing those green rounded helmets. The thought of fighter planes came to mind and guns, of course.

But what would it have really been like? For Dorothy's parents to have all their children leave and not know where they were and whether they were alive or dead. I've seen those old movies where the messenger shows up at the door with a telegram stating some loved one had died. But to *really* have been there and to have felt that loss. It must have been heartbreaking for so many people.

I now had a new understanding for Dorothy and everyone at the centre. I was wrong to presume that all older people had led simple lives and enjoyed only simple activities. Of course their bodies now restricted them from certain things, but many of their lives were rich and full of memories great and small.

Dorothy turned to me and smiled. "What are you thinking about? You have a great frown on your face. Have I upset you?"

"Oh, no! No, not at all! I was just thinking about how we live our lives in a cocoon sometimes and never really think about other people's experiences—what they may have been through or are going through."

"That is very true, my dear, and for you to realize that now will make you a very compassionate person."

I wasn't sure *exactly* what compassionate meant but I had a pretty good idea.

Dorothy then decided it was time to get back. I looked at my watch and realized my dad would already be there waiting for us. Maybe Dad and Dorothy could meet each other. The thought warmed me. Dorothy had taken me into a dream world of the past when she spoke and I loved it!

She held my arm firmly and we walked steadily back towards the centre. I could see my dad in the car and Tom was on his way out of the common-room doors. He must have just finished his visit with his partner, William. I was pretty curious to see how it had gone.

My dad got out of the car and came over to say hello. Dorothy seemed quite pleased to meet him and positively happy that he knew all about her. I walked her up the stairs and into the common room to her walker, which she'd left near the couch.

I asked her if she wanted to be walked right up to her room and she insisted that I go and join Tom and my father so as not to keep them waiting too long. I smiled appreciatively and leaned in to kiss her on the cheek. It was smooth and soft and she smelled like powdered flowers. She squeezed my hand firmly and kissed me back.

"I can't tell you how wonderful it was today to hear all about your life. It meant so much to learn more about you and also your husband."

"Well, dear, it is very special to have someone to listen to those old tales. I do enjoy talking about Frank because I miss him so." Dorothy sighed but still had a pleasant smile that made me feel she was, in many ways, content.

"Anytime. I'd love to hear more." And with that I waved goodbye and ran out to the car.

That night Tom phoned. It had been kind of hard to talk to him when Dad was in the car so I was really glad when

Jane said there was a call for me. We talked and talked. It seemed so natural speaking to him. I really hadn't had conversations with that many boys but I'd always imagined it would be painful and awkward. Tom was so respectful and sincere.

At the very end of our conversation Tom surprised me by asking if we might be able to go to a movie sometime. As soon as he said it, the butterflies that seemed to disappear the more I talked to him, came rushing back to my stomach with a vengeance and I revelled in the joy of it all.

I told Tom I'd really like to do that and was secretly pleased at the new material I'd have for my daydreaming life. Going to a movie gave me enough fodder to fill daydreams for at least a few days.

Tom suggested we go next weekend, maybe on Saturday afternoon. I agreed readily but secretly wondered how I could wait a *whole* week!

Chapter 14

On Monday we had our first weekly meeting of Match Made before Heaven. It was held in the gym, and as everyone arrived we formed small circles and sat on the floor. We talked about our partners and the party we'd had last week. Most volunteers had only seen their partners at the introduction meeting and had not had the chance to visit them again on the weekend as Tom and I had. In my group we discussed what their first impressions had been, what games they liked and how hard or easy it would be to find time to meet with them.

Then we got together in a big circle so that we could share ideas and so that Tanya and I could answer any questions the other students might have. Mr. French came and went during the meeting, checking on how we were doing. He knew we had a pretty good handle on the situation so he let us do our thing.

I spoke to the group briefly about my visit the previous day with Dorothy and some students had questions about her. I answered them freely and told them about her going to England as a nurse during the Second World War. I hadn't mentioned this to Tom yet and he and the other boys thought it was pretty cool.

I had asked Tom last night if he'd be willing to talk about his visit with William at the meeting. He'd agreed, so I turned to him next and waved him up to the front.

"Well, my partner is kind of ill. He has something called Alzheimer's disease. I phoned his son last night to find out more about it because our visit was kind of interesting. William does things like ask me a question, and then when I've answered it and asked him something else, he's not sure whether he asked me the question at all. He even said, 'Oh, yes, and who are you again, son?' to me a couple of times. It's hard because he can't remember the rules of most games and he's not really even sure about his kids and how many he has and everything. I guess he's been at the centre for more than ten years and has been living with Alzheimer's for that long. His son told me he was going to give me some more information about it so if anyone else has questions I might be able to answer them better after my next visit."

Tom sounded so confident. He was kind of soft spoken but he didn't seem to mind speaking in front of everyone. I liked watching him talk about William. Tom had compassion for his partner. It was something everyone in the group was beginning to understand.

I began to realize that Tanya had made an excellent match in William and Tom. Had she known Tom would be so willing to learn more about William's illness or was it just a lucky connection? Either way Tom would do well by William and bring pleasure to his life.

Some of the students had questions for Tom and then a few for Tanya as well. We finished off the meeting and reminded everyone to make their own arrangements to visit with their partners sometime this week. Match Made before Heaven would meet again in one week—after my next visit with Dorothy and my *date* with Tom!

Chapter 15

I was painfully patient all week. Tom was friendly in the halls and we'd chat sometimes during lunch. I was cool and collected and tried not to appear too obsessed about our upcoming date and our growing friendship.

School was going well and I was trying really hard to stay on top of my homework. Every one of our teachers kept saying that high school would be such a challenge. They said we'd be blown off our feet. "You'll be the little ones and no one will be responsible for helping you out except yourselves."

I'm starting to get excited about heading to high school, but at the same time I'm enjoying Grade 8 enough that I can imagine staying here forever. I wonder which school Tom will end up at for Grade 9.

The week finally came to an end and Friday after school Tom met me at my locker.

"Hey!" Tom's smile was going to seriously ruin my heart.

"Hi, how was your day?"

"It was okay. Yours?"

"It was good."

"I was just wondering about tomorrow. My mom said she can drive us to the mall and pick us up a few hours later. She has some errands to do anyway. Is that okay with you?"

"Yeah, that sounds great. I'm glad you didn't forget about it." Oh, God. Did that actually come out of my mouth?

Tom just smiled and said of course he hadn't forgotten. I think he thought I was teasing him.

"Okay then. We'll pick you up about 1:30 if that's okay. Most of the movies start at 2:00 or 2:30, so that should give us enough time."

"That sounds perfect."

"I'd like to walk you home again except that I have to go and babysit my little sister."

"Oh, that's okay. I'm actually meeting Tanya in a few minutes anyway. She's sleeping over tonight." Would he think we were too old for sleepovers?

"Hey, that's great. Have fun!" He was nice!

"Thanks. See ya!"

"Bye."

And with that he was gone and Tanya was grinning wildly as she came down the hall from the other direction.

"Are you ready to go?" She paused when I nodded and then said, "You better be ready to talk!"

I hadn't told her anything yet about Tom. After the meeting on Monday she knew that we'd visited our partners together and now she knew that he'd come to see me at my locker. I wonder how much of our conversation she'd heard.

We had a great walk to my house and I told her bits and pieces about Tom. She seemed genuinely happy for me and excited about the idea of a date. Tanya hadn't had a boyfriend yet either but seemed to know enough about dating because of her older brothers and sisters. She promised she'd give me pointers. I laughed and said it was an afternoon movie. I wasn't going to need any pointers. Was I?

Tanya and I rented a movie. It was a tearjerker. Sometimes I just love watching movies that make you cry. You feel so tired and drained of energy after it's all done. I like it when some character or story has affected me enough to create that kind of feeling. Especially when you have a girlfriend who cries just as easily as you do.

Tanya slept on a mattress on my floor and we talked until about 2:30 in the morning. We covered everything from kissing to marriage to divorce, but we eventually ended up talking about our club.

"I've been thinking about an idea for another kind of party thing at the centre."

I was feeling pretty sleepy at this point but I was curious about what she had to say.

"I was talking to some of the seniors at the centre and they love the students coming to see them. They were wondering about meeting some of the volunteers' families. I was thinking we could have a Match Made before Heaven family night. Everyone could bring their parents and brothers and sisters, and you and I of course would have to plan the whole party and food and stuff but I think it'd be fun." Tanya was always thinking.

"Yeah, I think that's a great idea. We could make little invitation cards and stuff. What about if the seniors could have their families there too?" It came out of my mouth before I'd even had a chance to think about it!

"That's great but I have no idea where we'd put everyone. That could really add up to a lot of people."

"Why don't we have it at school in the gym? It is a school club after all!" I felt like a genius with all these ideas streaming out of my head. Where *were* they coming from?

"That's great! We can either get the seniors there in the centre's van or we can ask that their family members take them there. Oh, it will be so cool. We can decorate the gym and get the whole club involved! I love this idea, Shelagh!"

"Yeah, it's very cool." I said this part sleepily, as I was barely able to stay awake. "If I fall asleep while we're still talking, I'm going to apologize in advance. I love the idea too but I can't keep my eyes open." I slowly reached up to turn off the light.

"Okay. Goodnight, Shelagh."

"Goodnight, Tanya. Sweet dreams."

Chapter 16

Tanya had piano lessons at 11:00 on Saturday morning, so we were up and she was gone before 10:00. I was tired. I just hoped I could make myself not look so puffy before Tom came to get me.

I wanted to spend some time with Jake so I told Betty I'd do his exercises with him this morning. I often helped Betty during the week in the evenings so I knew exactly the right order of the exercises off by heart. Jane was still sleeping and Dad was at work. A regular Saturday morning at the Howard household.

Jake hates his exercises so I try to make it fun for him. While he's lying on his back you have to hold onto one of his legs and gently pull it down. Then you have to try to straighten it for him and very gently push it back up. He hates it because he has no control over his muscles and can't help out at all. The idea is that someday, with the help of the exercises, he might be able to walk a bit with crutches or maybe even on his own. Right now he tries, but he really needs the support of someone holding him in order to take a few steps.

To make it fun I make up songs. They are really silly songs about nothing in particular, but they have a rhythm so that I can do the exercises to that beat. Sometimes I even add clapping or silly faces as if it's part of the routine. He giggles a lot, and even though it makes it harder to do the exercises, I love making him laugh.

The exercises take almost a full hour and by the end Jake is so tired he needs to take a rest, but I can barely carry him upstairs now because he's getting so big. When he was little I used to carry him everywhere. He'd grab onto my hair or my fingers and squeeze really tight. Sometimes he'd get too much hair and it would hurt but most of the time I loved the affection.

I took him up to his bedroom and laid him on the bed. He told me he thought I was funny and then rolled over to fall asleep. He'd only sleep for about twenty minutes and then he'd be raring to go again. I've never really been sure how Betty keeps up with him. But she always seems to manage.

Betty had lunch ready for me when I got downstairs.

"Jake's asleep already. I'll go get him again when he's had his nap."

Betty had Sundays off and Dad agreed to always be home that day. By Saturday Betty always looked close to exhaustion. She worked so hard I tried my best to give her a break on Saturdays.

"I won't be here this afternoon though." I hadn't told her yet about my date.

"That's okay. You've done more than enough this morning to give me a break and some sanity." Betty smiled. I felt good when I helped her out.

I ate my sandwich and wondered if I was wearing the right clothes for a date. Tanya and I had gone to movies before with a big group of people, but going alone with a boy was a different matter entirely.

Tanya had given me advice about what to wear and when I looked myself over I figured it would have to do.

Betty must have realized that she didn't know where I was going and so she asked, "Wait a minute, Tanya's already gone, so what are you up to this afternoon?"

"Tom and I are going to a movie. His mom's driving us to the mall and then she'll drive us home again." I really didn't need to say any more.

Betty smiled and again I got the feeling she was pleased that I was doing something social. She'd met Tom already and I guess she approved of him because all she said was, "Have fun!" She squeezed my shoulder and left me alone.

About an hour later the doorbell rang—it was Tom. Not that it was much of a surprise. After all I had been sitting at a spot by the front window where you can see out but no one can see in.

Tom looked cute. He really did. His short blond hair was sticking up in all directions and his eyes were piercing blue. They matched his sweater.

I called to Betty that I was going and then we walked down the front path to the car. Mrs. Braite said I should sit in the front and Tom could sit in the back. This made me feel uncomfortable. What did Tom's mom think of driving us to our date? Was she going to check me over and see if I was good enough for her son? My fears were put to rest when I took a better look at her.

She looked tired. Really tired like she'd been up all night. She spoke the same way. Mrs. Braite was not what I expected. She talked to me quietly and calmly most of the way to the mall and I felt shy. I didn't answer her questions very well. She asked me about my family, though, so I had to respond. I wonder what she thought of it all.

Finally we arrived and Mrs. Braite said she'd be back at 5:00 to pick us up. Tom and I went in the side door and straight to the theatre. We agreed right away on the movie. We bought some popcorn and drinks and rushed in because we only had ten minutes to spare. There were lots of seats, so we sat on the side on our own. I wondered briefly if we might see anyone from school.

I was kind of nervous about this whole thing and wasn't sure if I'd be able to enjoy or even watch the movie with Tom sitting so close to me. We shared the popcorn but had our own drinks. We bumped our hands once when we went to reach for some popcorn. *That* made us both smile self-consciously.

The movie was funny but neither of us laughed out loud much. When the movie ended, we left the theatre and I looked at my watch. I felt panicked all of a sudden. It was 4:45 and Tom's mom would be here at 5:00. We only had fifteen minutes left together.

Tom looked as though he felt the same way and led me around to the food court. It was noisy and crowded but we found a table for two and sat down.

We made small talk about the movie and the characters. Who'd been in what other movie and that kind of thing. We smiled at each other and we both laughed here and there. I really felt good with Tom.

I mentioned that we only had a few minutes left and he said, "Yeah, I know . . . THREE!" I laughed at the fact that he'd been keeping track too. It was really sweet that he noticed and it made me think that he wasn't going to let those three minutes go to waste! We sat exactly as we were until 4:59.

As we walked back towards the parking lot we started talking about next weekend. I said I wasn't sure but maybe we could talk about it at school. He agreed and we got into Mrs. Braite's car without another word.

Detailed questions from Mrs. Braite about the movie the whole way home almost put a damper on the entire afternoon. But when I waved goodbye to Tom and he hopped into the front seat, his sparkly blue eyes and his lovely smile made all those thoughts disappear.

As I walked up my steps I thought about Mrs. Braite. She seemed like a very sad woman. Everything she said had been said with such a sad tone. It almost overpowered her whole personality. I hadn't met her before today and Tom hadn't really spoken much about her either. It really made me wonder about moms.

Chapter 17

The next few weeks were a disaster. At our meeting on Monday Tom came to me and said he couldn't stay. He said he had to look after his little sister. He looked as if he was in really rough shape. His eyes were dark, and without his natural smile his whole demeanour changed. He looked a lot more like his mom.

"Is everything okay?" I was really concerned.

"Um . . . well. I can't talk right now. I've gotta go." And with that he turned and walked away, head down, out the gym doors.

I was stunned. I turned back to the group, which was starting to sit in a circle like last week. I looked at Tanya and hoped that she would be taking the lead today. All of a sudden I wasn't in the mood for leading a group discussion and Tanya seemed to pick up my vibe.

The meeting went by in a blur. Members shared their

stories of their visits with their partners. Tanya was great of course—encouraging people to talk and also answering questions when necessary. I just sat there trying to smile but really failing pretty miserably.

The next day was the same. Tom passed me in the hall, gave me a small nod, looked away and kept walking. Was it something I had done? Hadn't we gotten along well? Hadn't we said we were going to make plans to see each other again?

A few days later I decided I was going to have to make a move. I had to know if he was okay, if I'd done something wrong or if I could do anything to help. He'd cut me off without any explanation.

So after careful thought I decided I'd go to his house after school. Tom answered the door.

"Hi!" I tried my friendliest "you can talk to me" voice.

"Hi, Shelagh." Tom was still down. I could tell by the tone in his voice and the way his eyes searched the floor.

He had only barely opened the door. Was he hiding something or someone in his house? Tom closed the door behind him and stepped out onto his porch.

"Um, I've gotta get back to my sister." Tom looked at me hesitantly.

"Oh, I just wanted to say hi and see if . . ."

"Yeah, I'm fine . . . I guess." He cut me off before I could say that I was worried about him. "I'm really sorry

but I can't leave her for long . . . and . . . the stove's on."
He said it like an afterthought, as though it would give
him more of a reason to leave me standing there on the
porch.

I nodded and could only stare. What could I do aside
from grabbing him and shaking him and demanding
answers?

He stepped back inside and closed the door gently. I
felt rejected but I somehow knew it wasn't my fault. But
what could it be?

Over the next few weeks I tried and tried to talk to
Tom. I approached him at school and at the centre. I
even tried calling him at home. Mrs. Braite answered
and said he was doing homework and couldn't talk.

Maybe it *was* me. Maybe Mrs. Braite didn't approve of
me. Was it my family? I didn't live with both parents. I
had a brother who was disabled. Could that be it?

After that attempt on the phone I realized there was
not much more I could do. I had made a fool of myself
by trying for so long. Tom had rejected me numerous
times, but he'd never been mean or cruel. He had always
looked sad or just busy and preoccupied.

The problem was that I believed there *had* been something between us. Even Dorothy had commented on
being able to feel the chemistry. I was sure of it. I finally
concluded that there must be something else going on in

Tom's life and at this point he wasn't willing to share it with me.

If he just didn't like me anymore I would have to accept that. If he didn't want to open up to me I couldn't force him. I would just have to accept the fact that Tom Braite would no longer be a part of my life.

Chapter 18

As the fall passed slowly by, Dorothy and I had our weekly and sometimes twice-weekly visits. We talked, always non-stop, about anything that came to mind. I learned from her quiet manner and her graceful way of talking about difficult things.

She'd had a baby boy who died when he was only two months old. You could still see the pain in her eyes and feel it in her voice. It had been at least fifty years since the baby had died and yet the memory of that loss was still fresh in Dorothy's mind.

She had two surviving girls, well women really, Emily and Nancy. Dorothy spoke of them as though they were the most successful, respected women in the world. They likely were but I began to realize the pride a mother has for her children.

We talked about school and I told her I was doing all

right. I explained that sometimes I had a problem with daydreaming but lately I was really trying to focus. Dorothy made sure I understood how important my marks were.

Dorothy asked a few times about Tom. She wanted to know why we didn't come together to the centre. I explained to her the change of heart he must have had shortly after we'd gone to the movie together and how from then on things had been different. I told her it'd been pretty hard for me to understand what was going on with him and she agreed. She'd seen him with William at the centre so there was no question that he was still coming to see his partner. I was relieved to know that he was at least getting out of his house for something other than school.

In one of my conversations with Dorothy I went over in great detail how I had tried to see if he was okay and if he needed to talk.

Dorothy looked concerned and I wondered if she might just question him herself some day at the centre. Finally she seemed to accept, as I had, that he was in his own world now and that he wouldn't let anyone else in.

She helped me to understand the anger I had towards my mom and dad. Dorothy said it might be easier for me to see why I was so mad at my mom. My mom had left us and that's a pretty hard thing for anyone to accept. I agreed with her on that.

As we were talking, I realized the frustration I felt for my father was much more hidden. Dorothy thought I was probably resentful of him for letting my mom go, for not keeping up his side of the relationship and of course for working all hours of the day. I hadn't ever really thought about it like that before. And she confessed she'd never tried to analyse someone to such an extent before but was happy to give me any insight she could.

It did help. Seeing yourself through the eyes of a person you respect can bring a whole new perspective to things. I was grateful for her insight.

We regularly laughed out loud and we very often cried. We walked and talked and I learned a new card game. One day she pulled out an old cribbage board from her drawer and said she was going to teach me how to play. Once I understood the rules it became a regular part of our visits.

She had a special deck of cards that had really big numbers on them so she could see them clearly. At the beginning I thought she could have beaten me without ever seeing the cards at all. It took me a number of games to realize all the scoring chances, but once I did, I gave her a good run for her money. She skunked me for about fifteen games straight until I got the hang of it.

Dorothy wasn't really one to accuse someone of cheating, but a funny thing happened as we started to play and I began to realize her eyesight really was getting worse. Because the little holes on the cribbage board were so small she always made me peg the points. But she'd always check with her nimble fingers how many holes were between her blue pegs and then confirm how many were between my red ones.

I never cheated of course and she knew it, but every time I pegged, especially if I had a really good hand, she'd start fussing and putting on a big show as if I'd stolen the money right out of her pocket. She'd call foul and say I wasn't fit to play cribbage against anyone. She'd say I was cheap to be stealing points from right under her nose. And in the end we'd both be close to tears laughing about how absurd that idea really was.

It became a thing that she'd do. And as I got better and pegged out more often (that means that I won), I'd be ready for her response and we'd battle back and forth debating why and when I'd cheated. She always let on that I'd given myself extra points and eventually she'd back off by saying she'd never play again with someone she was so unsure of. And the next visit, sure enough, the board would be out and the cards ready to go!

As it started getting cold in early November, Dorothy decided she was going to teach me how to knit. Her hands were quite agile but she said it was too painful for her to knit something large. She wanted me to start with a scarf. She had yellow wool, bright yellow wool, and the needles all ready.

She was a very patient teacher and I was grateful for that. To have someone spend the time to teach a craft as intricate as knitting was extremely satisfying. I felt even closer to her as row upon row was completed. She beamed at me as I stopped dropping the needles and actually did a whole row with a new kind of rhythm.

She insisted that I keep the first scarf for myself. Although it wasn't my favourite colour I wore it with the greatest sense of pride.

I made two more. One for Dorothy, a nice rich navy blue, and one for Jane, black, just the way she would like it. I was proud that my hands had been put to work and wasn't sure I could wait until Chrismas to give Jane her scarf.

I loved my time with Dorothy and we shared many special moments. I could open up to her like I couldn't to Jane or Tanya or my dad or anyone. Was it because she wasn't family? Was it because she was old and wise? Whatever it was, I was grateful to her for being so open with me, for letting me talk and for teaching me a little bit about myself.

Chapter 19

Tanya and I had decided that the Match Made before Heaven family party could double as a Christmas party, so about a month before our school holidays we started getting organized.

At the end of November during one of our weekly Monday meetings we let everyone know our idea and told them to keep the date open. We'd have invitations for the partners shortly and other information would follow. Everyone seemed to think it was a good idea and Tanya and I were pleased.

We had a lot of things to do, so we decided to go out one night and plan it while we were at the local coffee shop where they happened to have great milkshakes.

Tanya took out a pen and some paper as soon as we sat down with our treats. "So we'll need to ask if the gym is available and check with Mr. French about supervision and all that. I was thinking that we should get some of the other students to join committees, you know, to do decorations and food and stuff. That way we can supervise and not be so busy running the whole thing."

"That sounds good. I'm sure they'd be more than willing to help out. Everyone seemed pretty excited about it when we told them." The students had looked at each other with smiles on their faces, thinking over the idea of their parents meeting their partners.

Tanya got a quizzical look on her face.

"What?" She had something on her mind but hadn't asked me anything yet.

"What happened between you and Tom? Is he okay? Everyone's kind of wondering about him. He rarely comes to the meetings and he seems so different. But I know he's visiting William because I've seen him at the centre. He goes every week."

"Oh . . . I know. It's really hard to explain because I honestly don't know what happened. We went to that movie and then *poof* everything changed. He totally cut himself off from me; he wouldn't talk. I was worried it was me but he's never really been mean. He just seems totally different, sad and confused all the time." I couldn't explain any more than that to Tanya.

"I wonder if there is something he could do for this

party that would make him feel better or involved or something." Tanya was always thinking.

"It can't hurt to try. If you can speak to him and see what he thinks that would be great. He is really hard to talk to these days, but I'm sure any contact from a friend would be helpful to him. Good luck." I really meant it. I'd tried and I knew I couldn't get through. Tanya and Tom were in the same class. Maybe Tanya would have better luck.

We sat and chatted about the party, the club and life at school. We came up with a huge list of things to do. Some we would do ourselves and others we'd try to get the members to do. I volunteered to do the invitations and I was really excited. I liked doing artsy things like that.

I went home that night and took out a stack of white paper. We decided that each invitation would be folded into four so that you could open it up. Tanya had shown me how to write the two halves in opposite directions so that when it was copied and folded you could open it and read it the right way around.

I must have drawn at least fifteen different designs before I got it right. I produced three versions that I was truly happy with and I put them aside to show Tanya before we picked one to present to Mr. French.

As I was sitting at my desk cleaning up my mess of

paper, Jane yelled to me that I had a phonecall. I went down the hall to Dad's room and picked up the phone.

"I've got it," I yelled down the stairs. "Hello?"

"Hey, Shelagh, it's Tanya."

"Oh, hey. How's it going?"

"Good. Um . . . I just wanted you to know that I talked to Tom tonight."

"Oh really? What happened? How'd it go?"

"Well . . . um . . . I think I know what you mean now about how he's acting. He pretty much said that no matter what happened he was *not* going to any family party for the club. He said that he had agreed to visit with William when we started this whole thing and he was committed to that but there was no way he was going to participate in our Christmas party. And that was it. He said it matter-of-factly and this time he actually sounded pretty angry. Like how dare I even suggest it. It was pretty weird, Shelagh. I'm really worried about him."

"I know. I just don't know what we can do. I feel as if I've tried everything and I have no idea where to go next."

"Yeah, well . . . I wanted you to know that I'd tried. I asked him if he'd like to play a song for the party. You know he plays the guitar like a professional?"

"Yeah, I know he plays, but I've never had the chance to hear him. Is he that good?"

"Yeah, he's really good. He's brought his guitar with him before to the centre. I heard him playing for William. William loves it. He can just sit and listen without a worry in the world. It's perfect."

"Well, I just don't get it. I don't know why he's so resistant. But we've both tried. As awful as it sounds I think we've done everything we can."

"Yeah, I know. I think we have too. Well . . . I'll see you tomorrow." Tanya sounded down even though she'd tried her best.

I hung up the phone and was tempted to call Tom, but I resisted the urge. I told myself that in his own time he'd come around. He'd see that we were trying so desperately to help him and eventually he'd appreciate that help.

Despite Tanya's failed effort I was excited about the party. I told Betty and Jane and Jake all about it, but I was especially excited to tell my dad. I told the others that they were all invited and that it was going to be a huge party in the gym with decorations and music and a lot of people. Jane, Jake and Betty would be able to meet Dorothy, and Dad would be able to see her again. I was so enthusiastic I could hardly sleep that night.

With only a week to go we had so much still to organize. I realized again how much I loved being in charge. I loved helping out the committees with problems that arose. I loved making suggestions and finding solutions.

Mr. French had agreed to supervise. We had booked the gym. The committees were well on their way to collecting all the decorations, food and equipment. Tanya and I had given out all the invitations, which I must say did look quite lovely. The only thing left to do was to confirm the numbers.

We agreed that all the students would check with their families and also check with their partners to see how many people would be attending the party. I had an official tally sheet so I decided to start with my family. Little did I know what a disaster that would be.

I went back to my bedroom with my tally sheet clenched in my fist. It wasn't possible was it? I shut my door quietly with only a faint click and sat on my bed. I took a deep breath. I did all this calmly because I knew that if I let myself go there could very well be some serious damage done.

This is what Dad said: "Oh . . . honey, the sixteenth? Is that right? Well that sounds like a really nice time. I unfortunately can't go but I'm sure Betty will be able to drive you and Jake and possibly even Jane if she's free." Then, of all the things to do, my dad smiled like he didn't have a care in the world and patted me on the head.

Didn't he know? Didn't he realize? This was *my* night. Everyone in Match Made before Heaven had been talking about it for weeks. Tanya and I were becoming like mini-heroes in our school. Everyone who wasn't in the club wanted to be and everyone who *was* in the club was gloating that they'd volunteered so early on. Didn't Dad know this? Didn't he understand?

I looked down at my hand and realized the tally sheet was now a sweat-covered crumpled mess. I didn't know what to think except that I was mad. What could he possibly have to do that was more important than this? I was bound and determined to find out—partly because he hadn't offered the information in the first place and partly because I wanted to know why he would miss this special night.

Chapter 20

The only person I could talk to was Jane. Would she care or even understand why I was upset? I didn't want this to ruin the whole party for me but I was starting to think it would. Of all the times for Dad to say "Sorry, I'm busy," this should not have been one of them.

I knocked on Jane's door.

"Yeah?"

"Hey, Jane. It's me. Can we talk for a minute?"

"Yeah, come on in." I couldn't tell if she sounded welcoming or not. I slowly opened her door.

"Are you going to be able to make it on Friday night?" I figured if I knew what her plans were, I'd be able to decide what angle to take with Dad.

"Yeah, I think so. It sounds kind of cool. Calvin, Tanya's brother, is going so I figure it can't be that bad."

At this she smiled. She was teasing me in the fondest way she knew how.

"Oh. That's good. Thanks."

"So what's up?"

"Well, I was kind of wondering if you know why Dad isn't going."

"Yeah, I know why. Don't you?"

"No!" Was she kidding? Of course I didn't know. Dad hadn't had the courtesy to tell me why he wasn't going to be there.

"Well, I don't think it's a big secret. He told me the other night when he picked me up from school."

"Okay. So? What is it?"

"Why are you so upset about this? It's not a big deal."

"Yeah, I know, but I'm kind of mad that he's not going. It's really important to me and I don't think he realizes that. I just can't figure out what would be more important for him than this."

"Oh, I get it. Well, maybe you won't be so happy then. He's going on a date!"

"What? Are you joking?"

"Nope. He told me he'd arranged it a couple of weeks ago. It's some lady from his office. She's in the middle of a custody battle for her kids, so he's been trying to support her *as a friend*." Jane had a sneer on her face. She clearly did not believe that that was the extent of their relationship.

"I don't want to hear any more. Thank you for letting me know. I'm glad you told me." I sounded childish. I sounded like I was hurt and was trying very badly to cover it up. I turned to leave Jane's room.

"Wait, Shelagh, before you go. What about asking Mom?"

"No. She wouldn't understand how much this means to me. I'd rather not have to worry about her being there and everything she'd have to say about it later."

I walked out and shut the door behind me. How could he? I'd told him about this party with plenty of warning. And now "some lady from the office" was going to ruin the whole thing. I could scream.

Maybe he would change his mind. He could always come after they'd had their little date. Oh, God, but what if he brought her? That would be worse than his arriving late and alone. I was just going to have to accept the fact that my dad didn't love me and didn't care. That was going to be a very hard thing to do!

Chapter 21

Tanya and I stayed after school with the other club members to get ready. We all brought a change of clothes to put on once the decorations were up and the food was out. I was determined to enjoy this and not let my father's absence spoil my evening.

Everyone was there except Tom. It was obvious to me but the others didn't seem to notice. William had expressed an interest in attending the party, so Tanya had arranged for him to come with his son, even though Tom wouldn't be there.

Tanya's family would *all* be coming. Tanya's oldest sister, Mary, had her licence and agreed to drive. Mary, who was twenty-two years old and just finishing college, often drove her little brothers and sisters around.

The other seniors whose family members weren't coming would get a ride with Mr. and Mrs. Miller in the centre's van. This included Dorothy. She had asked her daughters but they wouldn't be able to make it. She told me they really did want to come but one daughter lived out of town and the other had an office Christmas party that had been planned for ages.

Tanya and I looked around the gym for one last inspection. It looked great. The students had done such an amazing job. Now it was time to get changed and get ready to greet the guests.

Tanya and I walked into the change room with our knapsacks. It was kind of eerie being in school on a Friday night. As we got into our nice clothes, Tanya asked if my dad was going to be there. I must have given her dagger eyes because she literally jumped back.

"No, he's not coming and I'd be happy to talk about it another time, but right now I really don't want to get more upset and have it ruin my evening. I'd rather just leave it be."

Tanya looked genuinely surprised. She also looked like she knew that I needed some unconditional friendship tonight and she was prepared to give it to me.

"Shelagh, this has been our thing. And we should have fun tonight no matter what happens. Let's go out there and show everyone why and how this club has become such a wonderful success!" Tanya smiled.

Her smile and her attitude inspired me. There was no way I was going to let my dad ruin this for me just because he wasn't going to be here for it. Well, I'd have to convince myself of that for at least the next few hours anyway.

We walked together to the front door of the school. We'd be helping the seniors out of the cars as they were dropped off. As I looked up and across the street I realized that I was looking straight onto the porch of Tom's house. The lights were on inside but the curtains were drawn and I couldn't see anyone moving around. Was it possible that he might just come over for a quick visit? William was going to be here after all. I'd have to keep my eyes open just in case.

One of the first cars to arrive was the van from the centre. Mr. and Mrs. Miller pulled up at the front door of the school and started to unload the passengers. Tanya and I walked or pushed each one up into the school. Dorothy waited for me so that I could bring her in last. I walked her right into the gym and found her a seat near the food.

She gave me the warmest smile that said everything I needed to hear. The room, the atmosphere and the people were all perfect. I gave her a kiss on the cheek, squeezed her hand and said I'd be back with my family when I found them.

As more guests started to arrive, the gym began to fill with noise. I was relieved to notice that people were not shy. They were introducing each other, talking and laughing.

Betty arrived with Jane and Jake and they made their way inside. Jake had a wheelchair for occasions like this but he had refused to use it. Betty patiently walked him all the way in and sat him on one of the chairs we had set out for the seniors. I told them I'd be back in a moment to introduce them to Dorothy.

Tanya and I waited at the front doors until we were pretty sure everyone had made it in. We walked back to the gym and were amazed at how many people were there. I'd done the tally and we'd come up with about eighty people. I'd assumed that when it came down to it a lot would back out or not be able to make it. But from what I could see, the opposite had happened and I hoped and prayed we wouldn't run out of food. The room was full of life, packed with people standing and talking, eating and drinking.

I walked over to Betty and Jake. Jane had wandered off to find Calvin. I took Jake's arm and we made our way over to Dorothy. I started making up sentences of introduction in my head. I was so excited to introduce them. Betty brought Jake's chair with her and set it down right next to Dorothy.

"Dorothy? This is Betty and this is my brother, Jake." I beamed and thought briefly how proud I was of my little brother.

"Well, hello, my dear." Dorothy reached for Jake's hand and gave it a good squeeze. I'd told Jake all about Dorothy and so he grinned and rolled his head around to show how pleased he really was.

"And, Betty, I've heard an awful lot about you." Dorothy reached for Betty with her other hand.

"And I you. It is a true pleasure to meet you." Betty was wonderful. If I'd wanted a mother figure to accompany me tonight I couldn't have asked for anyone better.

Betty pulled up a chair beside Dorothy and they began to chat. I stood watching in awe as they started into a very long and in-depth conversation. I leaned in and asked Jake if he was hungry. He nodded so we went over to get some food.

As we got in line and I reached for a plate, I heard Mr. French call my name. I turned around and was greeted by a very beautiful woman standing right next to him. This must be his wife. He introduced us. I shook her hand and tried my best to smile. The good thing was it appeared as though Mr. French was really proud to be introducing *me* to her. I pulled myself together and introduced them both to Jake who seemed to love meeting all these new people.

We got our food and went back to Betty and Dorothy. Betty told me to go and mingle and make sure everything was okay and she would help Jake with his food. I asked Dorothy if she wanted anything and she said she was fine and urged me to enjoy my party.

I found Jane and Calvin standing in a corner. They seemed to be having a very serious conversation so I decided I'd bug her later on about meeting Dorothy. I made my way through groups of people and smiled at students who were doing their best to maintain conversations with their partners' families. At the same time some of them seemed to be trying to check on their partners and make sure their own parents weren't doing anything embarrassing.

There were a surprising number of little kids around and I was happy for them to see how great their older brothers and sisters were.

Finally I saw Tanya walking towards me. It was time to do our thing. We would officially introduce ourselves, all the volunteers and our partners and welcome the guests.

I walked back to get Dorothy and as we made our way gingerly to the front of the gym people began to hush. We had a microphone set up on the stage and Tanya was already there signalling everyone to move forward. Slowly the students started to file towards the front with their partners. Those who could, walked up the small steps onto the stage, while the others stood or sat in wheelchairs in front of the stage on the gym floor.

Dorothy insisted that we climb the three steps and she reminded me of the first time I saw her. She looked regal, even elegant, as she ascended the stairs on my arm.

As soon as all the students and their partners had assembled at the front, Tanya began her short speech. When I glanced down the row of Match Made before Heaven members I was suddenly aware that William was not among them. Then from the crowd in the middle of the gym came a boy and an older man, arm in arm, step by step.

It was Tom and William.

Tanya began: "It is with the greatest pleasure that we welcome you here tonight to our school. We, as you know, feel very special about the new friendships we have formed with our partners. The seniors you see at the front of the stage today told me that they wanted to meet their partners' families and share this friendship with their own families. After much thought we decided a party was the best way to do that. From the sounds heard earlier we think this idea may have been a very good one."

Tanya was interrupted by a loud round of applause. She looked at me and grinned. We had never guessed *that* would happen. I was standing next to her and became slightly nervous when I realized she was done. I would have a role in the next part of the speech.

As we introduced ourselves to the guests, I caught a glimpse of Jake and Betty smiling away at the back of the gym. Then Tanya and I, alternating back and forth, introduced each student and his or her partner. It worked as well as we practised it and everyone seemed very pleased.

Tanya finished with a thank-you to the students for really putting it all together and a special thank-you to Mr. French for supervising and being so supportive.

"The party is not over yet. Enjoy your evening. There still seems to be lots of food, so please help yourselves."

As soon as Tanya was done, Tom disappeared. How was that possible? He'd been standing beside William at the bottom of the stage for the past ten minutes. Now they were both gone, lost in the crowd. I imagined Tom was returning William to his family and then he'd be off.

As we all left the stage the Christmas carols began in one corner. One of the students had agreed to play the piano for anyone who wanted to join in. We had handed out song sheets and slowly a large crowd formed around the piano.

Chapter 22

I was on an emotional high as the evening ended. Jane did eventually meet Dorothy and they talked for a while. Tom did disappear but at least he'd been there to show off his partner. Betty took Jake and Jane home and then came back to get me when I was finished cleaning up. Tanya and I had given each other a huge hug. Her family must be so proud of her. The club had been her idea, and along with a little help from me, she'd made it into a very big deal.

I went to bed after thanking Betty a hundred times just for being her. I tried not to think about my dad missing the evening but I was reminded when I discovered he wasn't even home yet from his date.

I went to see Dorothy again on Sunday and she was beaming. We hadn't had a good chance to talk before we said goodbye on Friday night so I was curious to know what she thought of the party. Dorothy was very impressed, to say the least. The only thing she regretted was that her daughters couldn't have been there. She said that if she'd known it was going to be so big and success- ful *and* that she'd get to go up on stage, she'd have insisted that they be there.

I simply smiled and said, "Next time?"

She nodded and said, "Definitely!"

We sat in her room and played two games of cribbage before going for a walk around the inside of the centre. It was bitterly cold out and Dorothy was feeling weak of heart. I worried about her and couldn't bear the thought of losing her. I knew each visit was precious but it was still hard to imagine that someday she would no longer be around.

As I went to leave, Dorothy pointed over into the common room. Tom was sitting on the couch playing his guitar. William was in the rocking chair next to him with his eyes closed, rocking back and forth. Tanya was right, Tom *was* like a professional. He was playing some melancholy song that made me feel terribly sad. Sad for what I didn't know but the feeling was overwhelming.

I kissed Dorothy goodbye and told her I'd see her during the week. We hugged and then I helped her into a chair in the corner so she could listen to Tom's beauti- ful, sad music.

I went out the front door to see if Betty was there and I saw my dad sitting in his car parked in front of the centre. This wasn't right. I had pleaded with Betty for her to come and get me even though it was her day off. I couldn't stand the thought of talking to my dad yet. I was still too angry. I might say something that I'd regret.

Dad was supposed to be with Jake today. I didn't want to talk to him or even see him. He still hadn't told me himself why he missed my party.

Dad said cheerfully, "Hi, honey! I told Betty to make sure she had a relaxing day off and that she didn't need to come and get you. She put up a bit of a fight but eventually she gave in. How's Dorothy?"

"She's fine." It was all I could say. I was afraid all my anger might come pouring out and I wouldn't be able to stop it.

"That's good. I heard the party was quite a success on Friday night." Dad turned to look at me as he was driving so I folded my arms and nodded. I looked straight ahead. I don't know what I thought this was going to accomplish but I couldn't just pretend I wasn't mad.

Of course it was a success. Why wouldn't it be? Everyone else had their family members there to support them. More than eighty people made it a success. No thanks to you. These were thoughts I only dreamed of saying aloud.

"Okay . . . then." He didn't know what to say. Did he really not know that I was angry at him for not being there? Was he so wound up in his own personal life that he couldn't see how important it had been to me?

I wanted to make it through the rest of the ride without talking. I just hoped that my dad would too. I was angry and I knew eventually I wouldn't feel quite so upset. But for now I felt that my anger was justified and there was no reason why I should make the effort to talk to my dad.

It took three days and an explanation from Jane before Dad apologized. And for some reason, even when he did I wasn't satisfied. He seemed to think that he was in the right and that I should be happy for him that he had gone on a date. He apologized but it was forced and not sincere. I found it very hard to accept, let alone be friendly afterwards.

Dad was the one who was *supposed* to be bringing up a family. He was supposed to be supportive of his children and not going on dates when they needed him.

The whole situation was backwards, wasn't it?

I was not looking forward to Christmas. With only a few days left, plans for the day were still up in the air. Mom was trying to make arrangements to see us and Dad seemed to be resisting for some reason. Why hadn't they sorted something out long ago? The only things I had to look forward to were giving Jane her scarf and spending the day with Jake, who still believed in Santa.

Finally Dad told us that our cousins would be coming over in the morning to open gifts and then have dinner. We'd head off to spend the afternoon with Mom and Brad at about 3:00 p.m. My only consolation was being with Jane and Jake for the day.

Something had come over me and I was having trouble getting out of the funk that I was in. Usually this was my favourite time of year, but things had changed. I was pretty miserable with both my parents and my bad mood would make holiday time a disaster.

Dorothy would be spending Christmas Day with her daughters out of town and Tanya would be having a huge celebration at her home with her family. And to top it off, Betty was going to see her brother and his family for the whole week!

I wished Tom was around and I wished things were different. I wanted that feeling back that I'd had with him whenever we were together. I often dreamed of things returning to the way they'd been. In my low mood I was sure that was never going to happen.

Chapter 23

The holidays came and went. They weren't so bad and as I rested up and spent more time with Dorothy my spirits rose back to normal.

In early January as soon as we returned to school Tanya suggested that we pair up more students with seniors at the centre. Ever since the Christmas party students had been asking us about the club and wondering if they could join. There were many more seniors without partners, so we made plans to put the word out, have students sign up and then begin matching.

It was a great success and we managed to pair up another sixteen volunteer students with senior partners from the centre. We had an introduction party and then let the students make arrangements from there.

I felt content and like life was falling back into a groove when the dream that I'd been dreaming for months finally came true.

After school on a cold day at the beginning of February, Tom approached me at my locker. I was so surprised to see him that I jumped when I looked up and he was there. He looked terribly distraught, so much so that I was afraid to even ask him what was wrong.

"Um . . . hi. I know we haven't talked in a long time but I was wondering if I could walk you home." Tom looked worried, confused and upset. The only difference I could see from the past few months was that he was finally talking to me.

"Yeah, of course. Let me just get my stuff and we can go." Was he finally ready to talk? After all this time was it possible?

I had often imagined this day in my head. The day he might be ready to talk. I truly hoped that that was the case now. I grabbed my stuff as quickly as I could and shoved it into my knapsack.

We were silent as we left the school and I thought over how things had been for the past few months. I wasn't mad at Tom and it may have been because I'd never felt really hurt by him. Every time I'd tried to approach him he had always seemed distracted and reluctant to talk but he had never been rude about it.

We walked in silence almost halfway to my house. I wanted to start by asking questions but Tom was so silent I couldn't even think of where to begin.

As we passed by a park, Tom stopped and turned to face me. His eyes were the same intense blue. It was cold but there was no wind and his cheeks had become a bright rosy pink.

"Um, Shelagh, I was wondering if there were any more student volunteers who you hadn't matched up yet?"

"Well, no, I don't think so. But people are always asking us about it. We get newly interested students all the time. Why?"

"Well, I was wondering if you could find someone else for William." Now Tom looked even worse. It appeared as though hundreds of emotions were flowing through his mind.

"Um, yeah, sure I guess. The next person who asks can be set up with him. Is there a problem with William?"

"Oh, no! He's great. After talking to his son in the fall I felt much better about the situation. He told me the best way to approach him and talk to him and since then it's been fine. We have worked out a great arrangement and I really enjoy visiting with him. He loves it when I play him music. It's something I'm really glad that I discovered he likes." Tom seemed to be imagining a visit with William because his eyes looked distant for a brief moment.

Tom continued: "It's *me* that's the problem."

Tears formed in the corners of Tom's eyes and he looked away. I gently put my arm through his and led him into the park. There were swings behind some trees not far off. We sat down there. It was cold but I was now sure that Tom needed to talk. If I wasn't prepared to listen now it wasn't going to happen at all.

Tom looked at me and managed a small smile. It was an appreciative, thanks-for-being-you look.

"You're probably wondering why I never really spoke to you again after that time we went to the movie together, why I've been so quiet, why I refused to talk to you and why I've kept to myself all this time."

He pushed on without waiting for a response. "Well, the night that we dropped you off after the movie and my mom drove me home, my life changed forever and I've been kind of having a rough time since then."

I nodded encouragingly like I'd seen Dorothy do a hundred times.

"That night my mom and dad sat me down and explained something to me. My dad has a brain tumour. The doctors had already done some tests before my parents told me and they all came back with bad news. He is really sick. They can't operate and he is going to die soon."

He paused and looked up to see my reaction. I was wide-eyed and afraid for Tom and his family.

"So that Monday when we had our club meeting I was still pretty stunned. I couldn't stay. I needed to go home and the comfort of friends wasn't what I was looking for at the time.

"Ever since then it's been really hard. My dad has been in and out of hospital and my mom's been there with him most of the time. I've been trying to take care of Emma but she's only four years old so it's hard. My grandma's been basically living with us to try to help out." Tom gave me the smallest of smiles.

"Now my dad's at home. The doctors have only given him a few more weeks to live. Since there's nothing more they can do, they told him he might as well stay home and die surrounded by family."

Now Tom stopped. He looked up into the sky and blinked.

I reached over and put my hand on his shoulder. I squeezed gently and held on. What could I say? Nothing was going to make him feel better or take away the pain. I would have to be silently supportive.

"So I really just wanted to say I'm sorry. I cut myself off from everyone and it wasn't fair to you not to explain why."

"Tom, I should have asked you. I should have been there to listen ages ago." I sounded desperate but I felt terrible that he'd been suffering silently.

"No, no. You tried over and over again to talk to me. I was torn inside every time you came to me. It was my choice to deal with it this way. I just didn't know what to say. I didn't know how to explain to anyone what was happening to me."

It started getting dark so we both got up and kept walking towards my house. We were silent again until we got close to the front door. It was dark now and I shivered a little with the cold.

"Shelagh?"

"Yes?"

"Thank you for listening. I needed the fresh air and some time out of my house. You are really easy to talk to. Thanks."

A million words passed over my tongue and yet I was speechless. How could I ever tell him how sorry I was? How could I ever express how much my heart hurt for him? I should have kept trying and trying. I should have been there for him.

I looked up from my boots and his face was an inch away. Then slowly his warm lips touched mine. I closed my eyes and a warm sensation filled me. It raced through my arms and body and legs, right down to my toes. It seemed as though it might last forever when Tom gently pulled his lips from mine.

He smiled. I hadn't seen a smile like that on his face

for a very, very long time.

"Thanks again for listening." Then Tom turned around and began his long walk home.

I wanted to call after him but nothing would come out. I wanted to tell him to come back, to come inside, to hold me tight. But he was gone into the darkness and cold of night.

I walked up the steps to our house. I realized I was no longer cold. I was now filled with a warmth that did not come from my winter coat.

As I opened the front door I felt more confused than I had in a long time. I had adult problems and issues thrown at me with full force.

Tom had *kissed* me! That was my first kiss. Everyone always talks about their first kiss and I had just had mine.

But Tom's dad was dying. He wouldn't live for more than a few weeks. Isn't that what the doctors had said?

How could I feel joy at a time like this?

As I took off my coat and boots I noticed Jake. He sat propped up on some pillows on the couch. I wanted to grab onto him and never let go. As I hugged him he pushed away, wondering why I was so spontaneously affectionate. The thought of losing him was firmly in my mind and something I knew I could never bear.

How was Tom able to deal so well with this? After opening up to me, he hardly seemed to shed a single tear. Maybe his composure was just for show. Maybe he hurt so deeply he couldn't let anyone know how strongly he really felt. Or maybe his way of dealing with it had been to wait until he was ready. He had waited for almost four months before he was even able to talk about it. I was grateful that he had come to me.

The only thing I was sure of now was that I would forever be by his side when he needed me. And when I wasn't sure if he needed me—I would find out.

Chapter 24

I had a lot on my mind. Dorothy wasn't feeling well and Tom and his family were forefront in my thoughts. Now when I daydreamed it wasn't for fun.

At the end of math class Mr. French called me over to his desk.

"Shelagh, I've heard really good things about the new volunteers."

"Oh, yeah? That's good. Yeah, things seem to be going well." I knew I sounded distracted. I just hoped he wouldn't notice.

"Is everything okay with you? You seem kind of down lately."

"Umm. Well, I guess I am down." I paused to think about where to begin.

"I don't know if you know this but Tom Braite's dad is really sick. In fact he's dying and Tom just told me about a week ago. I've been going over there every day after school to play with Emma. She's four and I don't think she understands the whole thing. But with Mr. Braite home all the time there is kind of a strange feeling in the house. He can't talk or anything. He stays in a hospital bed they have set up in the den. So it's like they are just waiting. . . ."

The last thing I wanted to do was talk about Tom and his family behind their backs and the second to last thing I wanted to do was cry in front of Mr. French. But it appeared as though both were about to happen. Tears started streaming down my face and as I continued to speak the words came out in chunky sobs.

"And . . . I also . . . just found out . . . from Dorothy . . . last night . . . that she's not doing . . . so well either. . . . I guess her heart . . . is slowly getting worse . . . and I think . . . she's ready to go." I took a deep breath and in one shot said, "She wants to be with her husband."

I was *so* embarrassed. I had no control over my emotions. They just poured out and now I felt so stupid.

"Shelagh." Mr. French grabbed my shoulders and held on firmly, making sure my eyes were focused on his.

"I know it is really hard to see this now but the time you've had with Dorothy has been incredibly special. I truly believe that you've come into her life when she needed you. You are a very strong person and Dorothy knows that you can handle this." He paused and then started again.

"You are the best friend anyone could ever hope for with respect to Tom. What the Braites are going through must be devastating but your support, I'm absolutely sure, is priceless to them. To have your assistance with Emma would be to have every mother's and wife's dearest wish answered." Mr. French looked at me so sincerely.

I had heard everything he said. I only wished I'd been able to record it so that I could play it over and over again. He told me to go and wash up and to take my time. He would let my gym teacher know that I would be late for my next class.

How had everything happened so quickly? In seven months my life had gone from simple and dull to busy, complicated and emotional. And to top it off I think I may have also fallen in love!

That afternoon I met Tom as usual by my locker. I asked him if he'd mind if I didn't go to his house today. I was so physically and emotionally exhausted I needed to rest. He seemed disappointed but without hesitation said of course it was fine.

I was so tired I took the bus home. I just didn't have the energy to walk all that way. I dragged my feet up the front stairs, threw my stuff inside the door and crawled upstairs to my bed.

Betty woke me at 6:30 for dinner. I felt like I'd been sleeping all night. I had fallen asleep fully clothed and now my side hurt where my belt had dug into me. I rubbed my eyes and slowly started to go downstairs.

Betty stopped me and asked me to brush my hair and wash my face before I came down. She hadn't asked me to do that in years. I was thirteen wasn't I? I knew when I needed to take care of myself. Reluctantly I made my way back up to the washroom. I brushed my hair, washed my face and felt immediately refreshed. I decided I'd better change my wrinkled shirt as well.

When I came down the stairs it was awfully quiet. I assumed everyone had begun eating or was possibly already finished. I pushed open the door to the kitchen and heard Dad's voice coming from the dining room. Then I thought I heard Dorothy. That couldn't be. I must have still been dreaming from my nap.

I turned into the dining room and there sitting at the table was Dad, Jake, Jane, Betty, Dorothy and Tom!

"Surprise!!!" They all yelled in unison.

I put my hand to my heart for fear that it would stop beating. What, when and how had all this happened?

I smiled and stopped to look around. There was a seat left for me between Dorothy and Tom. I edged my way around the room and sat down.

"So we thought it would be nice to invite Dorothy over for a wonderful home-cooked meal. I called Tom to see what he thought and to see how much he could arrange and the rest is history. Let's eat!" My dad was in heaven, socializing, entertaining and making us all happy.

I had forgiven him a while ago but I think he was still trying to win me back. If this was how he was going to do it I couldn't be more pleased!

I leaned over and quietly cut Dorothy's meat. I knew from eating with her at the centre just how she liked it. And Betty had been smart to make mashed potatoes.

Tom would be happy to have a break from his house and to enjoy the company of another family for the evening. He was fast and furious into his dinner and I imagined he hadn't eaten well for days!

After dinner we all sat in the living room and had tea and cake for dessert. It was what I would have to call a lovely evening. That's what Dorothy said anyway. We had the chance to sit together on the couch and she told me quietly how lovely my family was and how hard it was to keep the visit from me.

My dad couldn't even have imagined how much it meant for me to have her there at our house. And to give Tom the chance to organize it all must have been a greatly appreciated distraction.

We dropped Tom off first and then continued on to take Dorothy home. I walked her up all the way to her room this time as it was getting quite late. She asked me to come in for a minute and said she wouldn't keep me long.

I had sat in her room knitting for what seemed like hours and hours before the Christmas holidays. It somehow seemed different tonight and I realized she'd organized some things and put others in small cardboard boxes. Was she really preparing for the end?

I looked around some more but said nothing.

"Shelagh, I'm afraid I don't really have much time left. I'm not sure how I know, but I do. I don't want to say goodbye but I also don't want to *not* say goodbye. This is very hard for me. Please know in your heart that whatever happens to me soon I will be with my love and that will make me truly happy. You have brought so much joy into my life. My dear, you have been such a good friend."

I had cried all I could this afternoon at school and I knew I had nothing left in me now but I was still overcome with sadness.

She continued: "I had such a wonderful evening tonight. To see Jake and Jane again and to spend time in your home was a small dream come true. And especially to see you and Tom spending time together. You are a great friend to him, dear."

"Dorothy, I don't want to say goodbye either." I made a quick promise to myself that I would stay strong and be positive. I wanted her to know, right then, how much she meant to me.

"Dorothy, you have changed my life forever. I will never be the same. Thank you for that." I leaned in to hug her and I thought she said, "I love you." It was so faint I didn't respond because I wasn't sure she'd said it at all. I squeezed her tight and then stood up to hold her hand. The smell of powdery flowers would linger with me as I left her there.

"Your dad is waiting, dear." Dorothy's face had peace written all over it. How could I be sad looking at her now.

I smiled my bravest smile and leaned in to kiss her on the cheek one more time.

Chapter 25

Tom had been through so much more than I had emotionally but he seemed to be able to deal with it better. Maybe it was because he had had the time to get used to and now it was a part of his life. I decided that I wanted to do something special for Tom.

He had finally come around at school and become his old self again. His friends accepted him with open arms and it seemed to be just the support he needed.

Through Tanya I found out who Tom's favourite musicians were. Tanya and I searched and searched to see if any of them would be in town anytime soon. After a few weeks we heard that a solo guitarist, one of Tom's all-time favourites, was going to give a concert in a small pub.

If they served food along with the drinks, we'd be okay to go. Otherwise we'd have to pretend we were nineteen, which both Tanya and I did *not* think was possible. We checked with all the parents involved, my dad, Tanya's parents and Tom's mom, to see if they'd approve of our going to this small but oh so important concert. They all agreed when we suggested Tanya's sister Mary accompany us there and home again.

It was to be a surprise for Tom, so I swore his mom to secrecy. In her quiet, sad manner she thanked me for keeping her son in good spirits.

Mary agreed to come with us to supervise. She was eager to help out since it involved cheering someone up. The four of us piled into her car and headed downtown for the big night.

Tom had no idea where we were going and I could hardly contain my excitement. He must have thought it was a girl thing that he was simply being dragged along to. He never guessed what we had in store.

We managed to get Tom into the pub without his seeing any of the posters advertising the night's event. We ordered dinner and Tanya and I grinned from ear to ear waiting for the show to start.

There was a very small stage set up in the corner. A guitar and a chair sat waiting for the musician to appear. Within moments of our finishing our meal we were treated to the most incredible look of surprise and joy on Tom's face.

The rest was a dream come true for me and I guess it must have been for Tom as well. I had really wanted to give him a wonderful surprise and I felt like I'd done exactly that. We sat for the next couple of hours listening to a man play his guitar like no other.

The only thing I wanted more than this was to hear Tom play his guitar. Despite the fact that we'd been spending a lot more time together we'd still never had the opportunity to just sit and relax for a moment to enjoy some music. I was going to demand that someday after school he play me a song—a happy song.

Tom was beaming when we left the pub. Mary seemed pleased that she'd been able to help out. And I was grateful to her for making the evening a reality.

Mary and Tanya dropped Tom and me off at my house. Tom said he'd walk home from there. Tanya gave me a look that said, "You better give me a call and let me know what this is all about."

I smiled and said thank you again to Tanya and especially to Mary.

I noticed it was getting warmer as Tom and I stood looking at each other in front of my house. It was pretty late but I had no interest in going in. I suggested we sit on the steps for a bit and Tom agreed.

"I have never had anyone do something so special for me in my whole life." Tom was grateful for what I'd done, but more importantly he was happy.

I didn't know how long it would last but truthfully I didn't care. At that moment sitting on my porch nothing could have changed how we felt. All I could think was how much I didn't want the moment to end.

Tom held onto my hands. His hands were warm and soft and I felt that rush through my whole body once again. He had some kind of electricity that he was able to pass on to me when we touched. I wondered if that was the chemistry Dorothy had talked about. I'd never felt it with anyone else and I hoped he hadn't either.

"I wanted to do something special. It really means a lot to me to see you happy." I knew he knew all of this but the hand-holding thing was starting to make me feel nervous so I started to ramble.

Tom leaned over and kissed me. This time it was a little longer and a little different. When he looked up at me again I knew he had to leave. It was late and his mom would be worried. I would have to dream of next time and hope and pray that nothing would change.

Chapter 26

A week after we went to the concert, Mrs. Miller, Tanya's mom, called my dad to give him the news. Dorothy had fallen asleep in a chair in the common room and had never woken again. The funeral would take place in two days. I spent most of the two days in my room. I was overcome with grief and I didn't know quite what to do about it.

The morning of the funeral, Jane had been more than understanding and somewhat comforting as I was getting ready. She'd offered to lend me her grey dress. It was long sleeved, with no collar, and it was a little too long but I was grateful for her kindness. I thanked her and noticed that she really did seem sympathetic.

As we arrived at the church, Dad pulled into a parking spot and I saw Tom walking in with his mom. Tanya would be here with her parents as well.

I wondered to myself what would happen now. This woman had had such a profound impact on my life. I didn't want another partner—ever. I didn't want to be part of the club anymore. Dorothy was it for me. No one could ever compare and she could never be replaced. Her smile was as warm as anyone's I would ever know.

My dad held my arm while we walked up the steps and suddenly I felt my face glow. I had the largest grin I'd ever felt spread across my face. Oh, how terrible! I felt guilty for smiling. Then I realized it hadn't come from me—it was without a doubt some kind of feeling I must have been getting from Dorothy. I hoped her family would understand if they saw me walk into the church grinning like a fool.

We entered the church and took our seats in the first open pew. The smile on my face faded quickly. Tom and his mom were two rows ahead of us. How I respected them for coming even though they were going through their own very personal tragedy. How hard this must be for them knowing they would be here again all too soon.

Waiting for the minister to begin was truly awful. I already felt uncomfortable, as it was the first funeral I'd ever been to. My dad had done his best to explain the whole procedure but I still felt like I was waiting for something special—a sign from Dorothy that it really was a funeral for her.

Just at that very moment, an older woman leaned over and said, "Are you Shelagh?"

"Hm?!" I was startled. "Oh, yes, I'm sorry, I am."

"Oh, hello, dear. I'm Nancy. I'm Dorothy's youngest daughter. It is a great pleasure to meet you. Mom told us so much about you, dear. You brought great pleasure into her latter days."

I smiled. I needed to hear that. I had meant something to Dorothy and I did feel it now. We were a special team and she had needed me.

"Thank you very much. I didn't realize she told you about me. Dorothy is . . . was a unique person. I'm very sad that she died. Every single meeting that we had was so very special to me."

"Well, I know it was for her as well. I wanted to find you because I have something for you. While we were cleaning out her room this morning we found something for you."

Her eyes twinkled a little like Dorothy's as she handed over a small wooden box.

I nodded and tried my best to smile through my tear-filled eyes. If I blinked they'd overflow onto my cheeks. I wasn't ready for a full-blown heaving cry. Not yet, not here.

"We'll talk more later." She smiled, squeezed my hand and headed up the aisle to her front-row pew.

I looked up at my dad. He rubbed the back of my head and gently said, "Open it!"

I was in a different world again. All that was around me ceased to exist. I held the box in both hands and slowly lifted the lid. Inside was one of her rings, a solitary blue stone set deep into the thin silver band. Neatly tucked under it was a letter—perfectly folded on thick white writing paper. I put the ring on my right-hand ring finger and felt a warmth go through me. I was almost afraid to open the paper as I hoped so badly she'd written something down for me . . .

This is what it said:

Dear Shelagh,

You have been a gift to me these past few months. I have treasured every meeting, every conversation and every silence. I know you admired my ring and also that you would never have accepted it from me while I was alive. I hope this finds you celebrating my life, not mourning my death. Please accept this gift with my love.

My health has declined further as you know and I'm afraid I will not get the chance to visit with you many more times. I know too that you understand my death as a step forward into the next level, whatever that may be. My dear Frank will be there and with me—we will be together again. Keep this ring always close to your heart.

A thousand thank-yous for your time, your loyalty and most of all your friendship.

Love,
Your friend Dorothy

The organ began to sing forth with great volume just as the tears began to flow. Dad put his arm over my shoulders and squeezed ever so gently. I silently sobbed, heaving and shaking, tears streaming down my face.

As my body tired I lay my head on my dad's shoulder and tried to get my breath back. The minister began and I was lulled by his soothing voice.

The cemetery was about a twenty-minute walk from our house. I asked my dad if it would be okay for him to leave me there and I'd come home when I was ready. He hesitated for a moment then told me to take my time.

Family members and other friends had long since left and I was relieved to finally be alone.

I sat.

Right there in the snow.

I didn't think I had any tears left, but as I thought to myself what a wonderful change had come about in my life the tears flowed again. I knew that my life would be different forever.

I was grateful for that. I closed my eyes and just felt.

In my new self, I didn't doubt my feelings as they came to me. When I sensed a warmth fill my body, I was sure that Dorothy was with me.

I would come back here whenever I needed that sense of peace.

I turned to get up and there standing alone on the road was Tom. He smiled ever so gently.

I walked slowly towards him, wiping my face with the last scraggly tissue I had and timidly smiled back.

He reached his arms around me—without hesitation—pulled me close and just held on.

I rested my head on his shoulder and wrapped my arms around his waist.

We turned together, he held my hand and he walked me quietly home.

Chapter 27

This is me. It's a picture I drew of myself for myself. It's early June now and we're getting ready for graduation. I decided I'm going to draw a picture of myself at the beginning and end of each school year. I'd like to keep them and someday show them to my kids or even my grandchildren.

Drawing makes me think a lot about how I've changed this year. I still see myself as pretty happy and I don't think my taste in clothes has improved at all. But what I've seen this year and what I've experienced has made me a young woman. I am no longer a girl.

Tom's father died in April. He died at home in his sleep one night. Tom and I talk about it a lot and we often spend time together babysitting Emma. She always asks, "Where's Daddy?" and somehow Tom answers in the most caring way that he is gone. Emma always looks confused but accepts his answer and carries on in her wonderful four-year-old way.

We had a closing party for Match Made before Heaven. Some volunteers are going to keep visiting their partners through the summer but a lot are going away and many are getting ready for next year. There are some really keen Grade 7 students who are going to take over running it and set up a whole new group for September.

As I roll my ring around on my finger with my thumb I think of my friend Dorothy. I am reminded of what she taught me and how much I learned. My sadness has been replaced by a solid, contented feeling that knowing her has made me who I am today.

"Shelaaaaaaagh!!"

It's Jake calling me wildly from his room. It's time for his exercises and I promised him we'd play the clapping game today.

Acknowledgements

I would like to recognize and thank my students, who have motivated, inspired and challenged me over the past six years. Without them I would likely have forgotten what it meant to be thirteen. I would also like to thank my editors Cynthia Good, Mary Adachi and Sandra Tooze for their kind suggestions and sharp eyes. To my sister Wendy for being a kindred spirit. To my brother Michael for being my mentor. To my grandparents (in memory, Poppa, Gan and Granddad and in life, Granny) for teaching me the love of another generation. To my friend Vanessa for her gentle ways. To my stepdaughter Tyler for her innocence and endless love. Finally, to my partner in life, Daniel, for being my everything.